PRIME TIME CRIME

2

PRIME TIME CRIME

2

Steve Liddick

Prime Time Crime 2
Published 2022
Printed in the United States of America

Copyright 2022
All rights reserved

ISBN # 9798832605845 - paperback

Cover image courtesy of
Canstockphoto, thomaspajot, and andreykuzmin

Cover by Joleene Naylor
Interior design by Chris Harris

Other books by Steve Liddick

Novels

Old Heroes
All That Time
Sky Warriors
Prime Time Crime

Gift Book

A Family Restaurant is No Place For Children:
  The Wit and Wisdom of an Uncommon Mom

Cookbooks

Campsite Gourmet
Eat Cheap:
  A Cookbook and Guide to Stretching Your Food
  Budget Dollars

Memoir

But First This Message:
  A Quirky Journey in Broadcasting

Essays

The View From Over the Hill:
  Reflections on a Life Well Misspent
Random Thoughts of an Average Madman

Available at www.Amazon.com

Dedicated to police officers everywhere who became cops
for all the right reasons.

**Reporting crime is their business
Catching the criminals is their pleasure**

<u>ONE</u>

A dark figure climbed into a battered pickup truck and drove slowly out of the dense woods. Nighttime was best for this kind of work.

It was a job that paid well and he desperately needed the money. But guilt was eating at his soul. There were few choices for a man in his thirties whose only skill was stalking and killing the nation's enemies. There was no legitimate occupational group in civilian life that matched that job description.

He had two kids to consider and an ex-wife constantly pressing him for more support.

The children were his main concern and the reason he continued to do this damnable job. If he had any other choice he would grab it.

Lots of people hated their jobs. What he was doing made him hate himself.

<u>TWO</u>

The News Seven newsroom was waking up, taking on the buzz that would intensify as the city came alive and the important events of the day would be recorded and reported.

Stringers had already turned in their overnight video to be edited for the early and mid-day newscasts.

Coffee aroma wafted through the big room, staffers getting a jolt of jitters to jump-start their morning.

Always the first to arrive, Team Jerry was gearing up for what was to come.

Field reporting teams were named for their reporters. Jerry Harper, Cameraman Gary Mansfield, and Producer Katt Li were in their editing booth. It was a tight fit in the equipment-filled room with Jerry in his wheelchair and Gary, a robust six-footer, at the computer. Katt took up little space at just a tick under five feet tall.

The workday was headed their way in the form of a tall, thin man with the suggestion of a mustache and the shifty look of the kid who used to tell on everyone to the teacher.

"Heads up," News Director Stan Hawkins called out in a nasal voice as he rushed toward them through the maze of desks, computers, and squawking police and fire emergency scanners. He was waving a sheet of paper. "I have an assignment for you."

"We got lucky," Jerry said, just loud enough for his teammates. "I was afraid he was going to make us suffer one of his staff meetings."

Hawkins held the assignment sheet out to Gary.

Without looking up from his computer, Gary, with the longest arms of the crew, took the paper, passed it to Katt, and went back to editing a feature the team had shot the previous day.

"Alex Tucker is going to announce a new project," Hawkins said.

Katt also didn't look at Hawkins when she spoke to him. "What's Pretty Boy up to now?"

"Well, that's what you are supposed to find out, isn't it Ms Li?"

Hawkins turned and walked back to his desk.

"My, my," Katt said under her breath. "Aren't *we* snarky this morning?"

"Snarky is Hawkins' default setting," Jerry said.

"The setting of the permanently pissed."

Hawkins never got over being ignored when he ordered the team to drop its investigation of local Russian mobsters who murdered the city attorney. Especially when the success of the venture brought public and industry acclaim instead of the libel lawsuits he predicted. In Hawkins' judgment, the prospect of being sued trumped good investigative journalism. The investigation ended up with a lot of dead Russians, imprisoned public officials, public acclaim, and an Emmy for the team's reporting.

Katt scanned the sheet. "Little Alex is planning something that will mean jobs and tax money for the city."

"Tucker is featured in this month's issue of Carsonville Magazine as the city's Most Eligible Bachelor, "Gary said. "What's he got that I don't have?"

Jerry volunteered a suggestion: "A net worth of 200-million-dollars and his pick of Carsonville's young babes?"

"He doesn't have me," Katt said, fluttering her eyelashes. "Your personal honey-bunny."

"Like I said—"

"Shut up," Katt said, and smacked Gary on his arm.

If you went strictly by appearances, Katt and Gary were an unlikely couple. Gary, a large ex cop, Katt, a beautiful Asian elf, but without the pointy ears. Standing side-by-side they looked like Tom Thumb's little sister and Jack's beanstalk nemesis.

It took them several years of working together developing a great friendship and working relationship to act on feelings beyond the platonic. The matter was settled when Gary rescued Katt in a violent shootout with Russian gangsters who had kidnapped her. It was then they both realized there was more between them that needed to be addressed.

After that they addressed their brains out, so to speak.

Jerry was the youngest member of the team. He was paralyzed from the waist down, a gift from a drunk driver in a collision when he was in his teens. A handsome twenty-five-year-old, Katt and Gary thought of Jerry as a younger brother and respected his talent and work ethic.

Considering his disability it would be easy for Jerry to be bitter. The opposite was true. Although the reporting job had infected him with a certain degree of cynicism, Jerry was kind, considerate of others, and generally optimistic.

His close relationship with Katt and Gary was largely responsible for the optimism.

While he was still in college he worked as the News Seven office intern. He became close to Katt and Gary and they taught him about news writing, the operation of the camera, and video editing. When they engineered the previous reporter's departure, Jerry eased into the job and had since become the city's most popular TV reporter.

"Mount up, troops," Jerry said with a smile. "We're burning daylight." He laid the camera tripod across the arm rests of his wheelchair. Katt picked up her clipboard, Gary grabbed the video camera, and they headed for their satellite van.

Loading Jerry and his chair into the van using a special lift had become a smooth routine and the team was on its way.

The term "Team" could easily have been changed to "Family" in their case. They had been through a lot together and the three of them were as close as any blood relatives had ever been.

Tucker Tower could be seen from nearly every location in the city and could not be mistaken for any other. Eight-foot-tall white letters at the top of the thirty-story structure spelled out "TUCKER" for all to see.

They pulled up to the curb and parked with vehicles of competing TV stations.

As a major employer and a media star because of his high-visibility social and charitable activities, Alex Tucker could always count on a large turnout of Carsonville's print and broadcast media.

They rode the elevator to the Tucker offices on the top floor.

"I don't like the guy," Gary said. "He comes off as a snake oil salesman. Smoother than most, I'll give him that."

"He has his name on everything," Jerry said. "Tucker Apartments, Tucker Mall. Not just this building:"

"Lucky his name isn't Schwarzenegger." Katt said. "It would have to say, 'continued on next building'."

She snorted. Katt's laughs often came with a snort.

"There is something about him that isn't right." Gary said.

"His smile isn't really a smile," Jerry said. "His mouth smiles, but his eyes don't."

"Yeah," Katt said. "I noticed that."

Katt didn't miss much. A childhood in foster care had made her hyper-aware of her surroundings, alert for possible assaults on her self-esteem as well as her person.

Gary was a homicide detective before he quit in disgust over politics and inept upper management in the Carsonville police department.

"Lots of rumors of underhanded business practices," Gary said. "The public never hears about that."

"He has a hotshot public relations agency," Jerry said. "They cover up the bad stuff and crank out good stuff."

They stepped off the elevator into an enormous reception room. Original artworks lined the walls between floor-to-ceiling windows that beheld a magnificent panorama of the city to the west and the snow-capped Sierra Nevada peaks to the east.

"The carved walnut receptionist's desk cost more than my car," Katt said.

Gary chuckled. "A lube and oil change costs more than your car."

Katt stuck out her tongue at him. She drove an elderly Nissan rust-bucket.

"You could leave it unlocked and the key in the ignition and nobody would steal it."

"It gets me where I want to go. What more do I need?" That was pretty much Katt's attitude about everything. She did not own anything beyond what was absolutely necessary, including the clothes she wore: thrift store jeans, a T-shirt, and slip-on shoes.

Katt was a minimalist before minimalism was cool.

Gary was not far behind in that regard. His outfit was Dickies pants, a team T-shirt, and a fishing vest with lots of pockets for camera accessories. And extra handgun magazines.

They joined Carsonville's press representatives as everyone positioned their cameras and microphones at the opposite end of the room from the receptionist.

Security cameras covered every angle of the expanse.

A side door opened and Tucker's office manager, Kathy Rankin, an attractive blonde in her late thirties, stepped into the room. Rankin was what Tucker imperiously referred to as his "Chief of Staff."

With her was a mousy–looking girl of about twenty years old. Rankin was carrying a leather-bound folder from which she took news releases. She handed them to the mouse to pass around and then went to a lectern.

"Mr. Tucker will be with you shortly," she said. "He's on a call to Hong Kong."

"Well, lah-de-flippin'-dah," Katt whispered.

"She couldn't just say 'he's taking a leak'?" Gary said.

It was Jerry's turn to snort.

A few minutes later the door to the inner offices opened. Alex Tucker made a grand entrance. Expensively tailored and coiffed, he stepped up to the lectern.

"Is he wearing makeup?" Katt whispered.

The "spider sense" that some cops develop from day-to-day dealings with shady characters followed Gary into his new career. He always got that familiar tingle when Tucker was around.

"Good morning," Alex Tucker said. His smile was on high beam, a fortune in dental work on display. "Thank you for coming."

He waited a moment until all cameras and recorders were turned on before he began.

"The Tucker Development Corporation will soon begin construction on what will be our most ambitious project to date; three-thousand single-family homes in a planned community just within the city limits at the eastern edge of Carsonville. It will add thousands of taxpaying consumers to the Carsonville economy."

Tucker was media savvy. He knew right where to stop and start so editors could get clean sound bites out of his presentation.

"Sierra Estates will be economically beneficial for the citizens of greater Carsonville by adding to local businesses' prospective customer base. It will also offer environmental benefits. A large solar energy field will feed electricity into the power grid. The resulting savings will be passed along to residents of this community within a community. It will be aesthetically pleasing because all utility lines will be underground. The complex will have its own sewer and water treatment systems."

At Tucker's signal, double doors opened. Two large men wheeled a table into the reception area. On it was Sierra Estates in miniature.

Tucker used a telescoping pointer to indicate each of the features.

When he finished his formal presentation, Tucker took questions about increased traffic and crime, and the need for additional policing.

"What about the impact on habitat?" Jerry Harper said. "By bulldozing thousands of acres of previously untouched woodland, what's to become of all those animals that live there?"

Tucker became a little uncomfortable.

"Every effort will be made to keep as much of the natural growth in the forest intact as possible. Lots of small parks and green zones."

Jerry persisted.

"Mr. Tucker, isn't that like saying the animals that lived where homes are to be built will have to either find somewhere else to live. Or die?"

It was obvious by the wrinkled brow and pursed lips that Alex Tucker did not like the question.

"I am committed to assuring that the positives far outweigh any negatives that might be associated with the project."

With that, Tucker gathered up papers from the lectern said, "Thank you all for coming," and turned to leave.

Jerry was not going to let up.

"That really doesn't answer the concern."

But Tucker did not answer and left the room.

With no one to interview, everyone packed their gear.

On the elevator, Gary said, "Tucker's a dick, but that was a great idea."

"Why do you suppose the three of us don't like Tucker," Katt said, "when the rest of the city treats him like a God?"

"Because," Gary said, "most people are easily led around by their noses, but our experience has made us question everything."

Katt nodded. "Did you notice those guys who brought the miniature town in?"

"Yeah," Gary said. The type you'd see going at it in a bar fight."

"You don't need that much muscle to push a table around," Jerry said.

"Makes you wonder what else they do for Tucker," Katt said. "Considering what we hear about Tucker's business practices, this whole project could stand a closer look."

THREE

Everyone said how much Alex Tucker had loved and respected his late mother and father. He lost them both in a car accident just a few days after his eighteenth birthday. It was difficult, they said, for one so young.

Now in his late thirties Alexander Desmond "Alex" Tucker, Junior was handsome and charming with an engaging smile. He was a pillar of the community with an enviable investment portfolio, a successful business, and a history of generosity toward local charities.

What the public did not know was that Alex Tucker had despised both parents. His father had abused him physically for infractions of rules often made up on the spot. No matter what Alex did, it was never good enough and he would routinely be rewarded the boy with a backhand.

Not a day passed that his mother did not let him know in one way or another that his birth had been an inconvenience.

The wider world, of course, could not know what happened behind the closed doors of the Tucker mansion. Nor did they know that the abuse suffered by young Alex had created a Mr. Hyde that now lived just beneath the surface of a polished Dr. Jekyll.

Alex had spent most of his growing-up years thinking of ways to get rid of his tormentors, just as he did the family dog. His father had decided that a boy should have a dog. Alex didn't want the animal and resented being expected to take care of something he didn't ask for. He buried it in nearby woods. As far as Daphne and Alexander Tucker Senior knew, the dog ran away. Hit by a car and crawled off to die, they said.

They didn't have much time to think about it because a week later it was their turn.

The police report said they had both died instantly when their car swerved into the oncoming lane on a busy highway and went head-on into a fully-loaded semi. Fatalities all around. To accident investigators it appeared to be just another case of a driver falling asleep at the wheel.

Manipulation of the power steering mechanism on the senior Tuckers' Mercedes accounted for the "tragic" loss.

Young Alex was able to acquire millions of dollars in life insurance and Tucker assets. Over the years since, he turned that money into many more millions by building a real estate empire as well as enterprises the public and the law would not have approved of.

Alex Tucker was a psychopath and narcissist to the extreme, having no genuine feelings for anyone but himself. He was convinced that people existed for his purposes.

Unshackled by the curse of a conscience, Alex was able to make business decisions of personal benefit, even if he damaged or destroyed others in the process. And he did it with a warm and winning smile.

Everything was going Alex Tucker's way, free of the negative; nothing left but the positive.

<u>FOUR</u>

Seated at his editing station, Gary Mansfield was putting together the Tucker report that would air on the evening newscasts. Jerry had already recorded the standup open and close with Tucker Tower in the background.

"This is unpaid advertisement for Tucker Development," Gary said.

"The bigger you are, the more you get for free," Katt said.

"The newsmakers know we'll use the best quotes and make them look good," Jerry said.

"And get yourself in trouble with station management if you don't," Gary said. "Wouldn't want to upset the bigwig or make the audience cringe—and have them switch to another station."

"Why do we coddle viewers when we should be shaking them up?" Jerry said. "Let them cringe.'

"That's another thing," Katt said.

"Oh, no!" Gary said, raising his arms like he was fending off an attack.

"Not *another* thing," Jerry said, his hands to his temples.

"Shut up," Katt said and continued. "There are warning signs for everything. Wet floors, flooded streets, speed bumps. The population is treated like idiots. It's like people can't think for themselves; like we all have to be walked through life without any personal responsibility. I mean, can't you figure out for yourself that if you walk on a slick floor and suddenly go flying, then it was a wet floor and you shouldn't have been walking on it? If you're up to your ass in water on a street, the street is flooded. Duh. If there's a hump in the road you don't need a freakin' sign to tell say you shouldn't have been speeding through a neighborhood. You deserve what happens to your car. Your teeth will rattle and your suspension will be wrecked. Lesson learned."

"Businesses and government are afraid they'll be sued," Gary said. "They put up a sign for everything so they can claim you were warned."

"It's gonna be real different around here when I'm Queen."

Gary and Jerry bowed down.

"Hail to Queen Katt," Jerry said.

"What is the first thing you will do, your Highness?" Gary said.

"Do? What will I *do*?" Haven't you been listening? People will be forced to do it themselves. I will do *nothing*. I had a perfectly good tirade going there."

"And you were darned cute while you did it," Gary said.

"Sexist pig."

Katt was an astonishingly beautiful ice-blue-eyed mix of the Chinese mother and Caucasian father who dumped her in foster care when she was ten years old. She had well-earned anger issues. Katt could not have cared less what people thought of her or what she looked like.

After she and Gary finally got together, she gave up the habit of hiding her incredible figure under bulky clothing and her long, ink-black hair under a baseball cap. She had masked her beauty behind dark-rimmed glasses she didn't need. Now that she and Gary were an official couple she no longer used camouflage to ward off men who hit on her for all the wrong reasons. The fact that she was a martial arts expert capable of reducing large men to sobbing, bleeding, broken wretches was also a deterrent that could be called upon if needed.

"While waiting for your coronation," Jerry said, "we should take a closer look at Alex Tucker's development plan."

"Eek!" Katt said. "You mean do an investigative report?"

"Yeah, like that," Jerry said.

"That would make us investigative reporters," Gary said. "You know where that would lead?"

Katt said, "If we scuttled the project, the city fathers and mothers would be majorly pissed. They want those new jobs and tax money."

"Plus, Hawkins' head would explode."

"That's a good enough reason to do it right there," Jerry said.

They agreed to delay returning to the station as much as they could get away with when they finished mundane stories and use the extra time to look for real news.

Hawkins often complained about how long it took them to do their stories.

Katt's response: "You wouldn't go into a restaurant, order a meal and complain thirty seconds later that your dinner hadn't come yet, would you, Stan? Quality takes time."

That evening, when introducing the Tucker package on the early newscast, anchors Melissa Hallowell and Kyle Redmond read what Katt had written for them.

Melissa was a generically attractive blonde on the cusp of aging out. The public was not aware that off-camera she was a screaming shrew. One more wrinkle and she would be on the unemployment line.

Kyle was on the sunny side of retirement age; white-haired, not especially bright but fatherly and supremely self-confident. He could have the job until the day before his funeral. Together they offered the viewing audience the appearance of a warm and fuzzy news source.

Katt, Gary and Jerry watched on the control room monitor.

"A bitch and a moron posing as the world's greatest authorities," Katt said.

"What exactly do Melissa and Kyle do here?" Jerry said.

"They link together everything other people have done for them," Gary said. "Neither of them would recognize news if it bit them in the ass."

"And they strut around like they bleepin' knew what the bleep they were doing," Katt said. "It's what happens to a person when too bleepin' many people tell them how bleepin' wonderful they are."

In the years Gary had known Katt he encouraged her to remove much of the salt from her language. Where she might once have been perfectly comfortable in conversations with sailors and lumberjacks, Gary had succeeded in bringing her around to something that did not offend church ladies and frighten small children.

"In England they call those people 'news readers'," Jerry said.

If Katt lacked some of the social graces, she did have a gift for boiling complex issues down to their essence.

"In Carsonville," Katt said, "we call those people arrogant assholes.

<u>FIVE</u>

The next morning's newspaper featured a two-page color spread of the map of Alex Tucker's proposed development. It highlighted all of the luxury trimmings that would be available to residents of the planned community.

The News Seven editing booth's land line was buzzing when Gary arrived at the station.

"Mansfield."

"You the guy did the story about the Tucker project?"

"Our team did, yeah. Why?"

"Something you ought to know."

Katt came through the door, with Jerry close behind. Gary closed the soundproof door behind them and put the call on the speaker.

"The rest of the team can hear you. Go ahead."

"Parts of the acreage Tucker wants to build on are contaminated."

"Contaminated how?"

"Years of dumping hazardous wastes out there."

"How do you know this?"

"Because I'm the guy who dumped a lot of it."

"Why in God's name would you do that?"

"I worked for one of Tucker's companies and they ordered me to do it. I got kids to support. Not a lot of good-paying jobs for somebody like me."

"And you are telling me this because—"

"Because it's been eating away at me ever since. I have found another job. Doesn't pay as much, but maybe I'll be able to shave in the morning without having the devil looking back at me from the mirror. I guess they have some other poor sap doing the dumping now."

"You willing to say all that on camera?"

"Not a chance."

"Then it's a case of 'he said, he said' and proves nothing."

"But you can prove it yourself when I tell you where it is."
"Will you take us there?"
The caller paused for a long, thoughtful moment.
"Only if you promise not to film me or identify me."
"Why all this secrecy?"
"Because Tucker kills people. Or he disappears them, which is the same thing."
A stunned silence.
"You still there?"
"Yeah," Gary said. "That's what we call burying the lead. Murder would be an even bigger story than dumping poisons into the soil."
"I might be able to prove that, too."
Gary had to force himself to breathe. "Okay," he said finally. "No video, no names. When and where?"
"It'll have to be at night."
"Tonight's good. You?"
The caller agreed and gave them a time and place to meet. Jerry and Katt nodded.
"How do we get in touch with you?"
"You don't. I'll call you."
Gary gave the caller his cell phone number and the man hung up.
"How do we know this guy is legit?" Katt said. "He could be Tucker's man waiting out there for us. Tucker sure didn't like Jerry's questions at the news conference. And we do have a reputation for slaying dragons."
"The meeting is in the boonies," Jerry said. "I won't be able to get around out there. You guys can fill me in tomorrow. That is, if you don't get ambushed."
"I think he sounds okay." Gary said. "It's a chance we'll have to take if we're going to do this. The challenge would be to get proof without raising red flags that we're doing it."
"This guy is scared of Tucker," Jerry said. "It sounds like there are others who might have reason to be cautious."
Katt had some doubts. "But will they bad-mouth a man who could destroy them?"

"Let's find some contractors who have worked for Tucker," Jerry said. "See what they have to say,"

The team called companies with services and products of the kind Tucker's company would use and asked them if they ever did business with him. The hard part was getting anyone to say anything negative. It was obvious in their conversations that many of those they talked to did not like the man. Some went so far as to say they would never work for him again, but all hesitated to reveal anything more.

Finally, one subcontractor who was assured that whatever he said would be held in confidence decided to open up.

"He's a thief," Harvey Littleton said. "I won a bid a few years back to install heating and air conditioning systems on one of Tucker's projects. When it came time to get the final payment, Tucker wanted to renegotiate the price."

"Didn't you have a contract?" Gary said.

"Sure, but Tucker said I wouldn't get any future jobs from him if I didn't discount what I had already completed. I didn't want any more work from him if that's the way he did business."

"What did you do?"

"I refused. The job wouldn't have been worth it if I'd taken a cut."

"Then what happened?"

"Turns out I wasn't working for Tucker Development. The contract was with a corporation under another name. He declared bankruptcy with that one. Not only did I not get the contracted amount, I got nothing. Some of the other contractors got shafted, too."

"You're still in business," Jerry said.

"Barely. It's taken me a year to get halfway back on my feet again. Some of the others weren't as lucky. They lost everything."

"How much did you lose?" Katt said.

"Over forty thousand dollars."

"What you've told us will stay between us, but it would be great if you would agree to be interviewed."

"The only way I'd do it is if others who lost money would speak up. He can still hurt me by threatening my suppliers. Also, he sues people for little or nothing. I might win, but fighting it in court would cost money I don't have. He knows that."

They would keep Littleton in mind for future interviews. Once owners of other companies heard the story he told them, some opened up and had similar experiences and similar reservations about going public.

"At the rate Tucker is screwing subcontractors," Gary said, "soon no one in the city will want to work for him."

"What are we gonna do?" Katt said.

"Can't put it on the air without evidence or testimony to back it up." Jerry said. "His high-priced lawyers would shred us in court. Even worse, that would mean Stan Hawkins was right and I'd really hate that."

"We'll keep trying," Gary said. "Walk around in a cow pasture long enough and you're bound to step in something."

"Eeeoooooooo," Katt said.

"Gotta get The Shadow involved."

When the team took on the Russian mob they called each other by super hero names. Katt was Wonder Woman, Gary was Superman, Jerry was Captain Marvel, and Gus Tovar was The Shadow. Their go-to computer geek, Gus worked his research magic behind the scenes to get the dope on the crooks. Since his work often skimmed the fringes of legality, he didn't want any publicity.

"Gus loves getting dirt on the bad guys," Jerry said.

Gary punched in a number on his cell phone.

"Gustav, it's Gary."

"Hey buddy, que pasa?"

"Got a project you might want to get involved with."

"Not gonna get me almost killed like the last time is it?"

The Russian mob came very close to murdering Gus for his help in their investigation.

"What do they say? Close only counts in horseshoes and hand grenades."

"That guy woulda killed me if Katt hadn't kung Fu'd the crap outta him."

Katt had sneaked up behind the killer and unloaded some of her martial arts on him.

"No, this will be a routine research job."

"Uh huh. Why am I suspicious?"

"Why don't we come by your place and talk about it."

Gus Tovar lived and worked in what looked like an abandoned building in the Carsonville warehouse district. The brick-faced structure appeared demolition-ready, but was actually a false front for the computer genius's plush living quarters and workplace.

Team Jerry got a boring soft news assignment out of the way quickly and stopped by Gus's lair on their way back to the station. They parked the satellite van on the street in front of Gus's covert quarters.

Getting to the entrance to his place involved pulling back a panel in the chain link fence that surrounded his cluttered adjoining lot. They made their way to a boarded up entrance that hid a steel door.

"Why doesn't Gus live like normal people?" Katt said.

"If Gus was normal he couldn't do what we need him to do," Gary said.

"Kinda makes you wonder about us, huh?" Jerry said.

Gary found a hidden button, pushed it and looked up at disguised security video cameras so Gus could see them. Moments later they were buzzed in to stairs to the second floor.

With Katt on one side of Jerry's wheelchair and Gary on the other, they carried him up the steps. Even though Katt was small, daily physical workouts made her incredibly strong.

When they emerged at the top of the stairs the scene transitioned from the absolute filth on the outside to the unbelievable grandeur on the inside. Gus's living and work space had carpeted floors, paneled walls lined with original artworks by Mexican artists; all of the amenities of a luxury apartment.

"Hola," Gus said as they entered his inner sanctum.

Handshakes and man-hugs for Gary and Jerry. Little Katt practically disappeared inside a hug by the big man.

"Easy, Gus," Katt said. "I'm breakable, you know."

"Ha! This is the toughest woman I have ever known. Try to break her and the guy's relatives won't be able to identify what's left of him."

Gus witnessed Katt's fighting abilities when the Russian thug tried to shoot him. Skills few were privileged to be made aware of. Unless, of course, they were on the receiving end.

"Okay, what do you need my help with?"

Gary explained.

"Alex Tucker? Are you crazy? The guy is Carsonville politicians' personal ATM machine."

"He's that and more," Gary said. "He may also be a killer."

"Is that supposed to give me confidence to help you guys?"

"Nobody will know."

"That's what you said the last time and look what happened. Almost."

"We need a list of companies Tucker owns and what they do," Gary said. "Any dirt you can dig up would also be good."

It took a little coaxing to convince Gus to join the hunt. In the end, his hunger for action outweighed his fear of retaliation. It rarely takes much effort to get an adrenalin freak to jump into a whirlwind.

With Gus solidly on the team, they went back to the TV station.

The three huddled in the editing booth. A plan was beginning to take shape.

"While Gus is trying to hack Tucker's cyber world," Gary said, "Jerry will try to find some more people who have done business with the guy. Katt, you and I will meet with the whistleblower tonight to see if he's got something on Tucker—or if he's full of beans."

They had not noticed that the news director was standing next to their booth. "What are you guys up to," Stan Hawkins said.

"Christ, Stan," Gary said. "You shouldn't sneak up on people like that."

"A good thing I did. I heard the name Tucker. When you three get quiet I start to worry. I say again, what are you doing that could get the station in trouble?"

Seeing no way out of it, Gary decided to let Hawkins know as little of their plan as possible. But he did not mention their informant.

"We believe Alex Tucker is not the upstanding citizen and businessman most people think he is."

"Don't tell me you're going to go after Tucker."

"That we are. If we can prove what we are hearing is true, Tucker should be in prison, not on a pedestal."

"Well," Hawkins said. "You can stop right where you are. We are not going to get in the way of a multi-million-dollar project that will benefit the city."

"Even if he's a criminal?" Katt said.

"I don't believe that."

"No, Stan," Gary said. "You *choose* not to believe that. Maybe you should get into another line of work, since investigative reporting does not seem to appeal to you."

"My answer to that is to stop what you're doing right now."

"If that's the case, please accept my immediate resignation."

"If that's what it takes."

"Mine, too," Katt said.

"And mine," Jerry said.

Hawkins looked stunned.

"We will be freelancing this, Stan. We will take what we get to every news outlet in the city—*except* News Seven."

Jerry said, "Don't you think it's going to look strange that your Emmy-winning field reporting team up and quit as a group, Stan?"

"Because we'll be sure to spread it all around town," Katt said. "We'll be letting everyone know we quit because the news director wouldn't let his investigative reporters . . . you know, . . . investigate."

Hawkins was getting uncomfortable.

"That should shine a spotlight on your timid nature," Jerry said. "And have an effect on any future job prospects."

"Now just a minute," Hawkins said. "I can't let you endanger the station. Tucker is a big man in this town. We would surely be sued."

"You can't stop us, Stan," Jerry said. "We are going to do this story and we don't need your blessing."

"You forget who you work for."

"No, *you* forget who we work for. We work for the people of Carsonville and we don't have to be employed by News Seven to do it."

Hawkins went very quiet.

"I've done my part," he said, finally. "I warned you. If you go ahead with this it's all on you."

He turned and went back to his desk.

<u>SIX</u>

There was no moon to illuminate the wooded spot where Katt and Gary agreed to meet the man who claimed to have damaging information about Alex Tucker. Far from the noise of the city, crickets and katydids were the only sounds.

They were sitting in Gary's personal van rather than the highly visible satellite truck.

Gary brought his own video equipment, which was of better quality than News Seven provided. A small battery-powered floodlight would be good enough for anything he had to record.

Gary shone his flashlight on a sign that read, "The future home of Sierra Estates" above an artist's rendering of the future village.

Their would-be informant had not yet arrived.

"I'm gonna hate to see all this plowed under so Alex Tucker can add to his millions," Katt said,

A half hour passed and still no whistleblower.

Katt was getting antsy. "Have we been stood up?"

"Give it a little more time."

A short while later there was a light knock on the side of the van that startled them both.

Gary rolled down the driver's side window and turned his flashlight on the source of the knock.

"Where the hell did you come from," Gary said to a large man he estimated was in his early thirties standing next to the van.

"Been here awhile," the man said quietly. "Wanted to make sure you were alone."

Gary recognized the voice as the man who had called earlier. He did not relax his grip on the Makarov 9mm semi automatic handgun in his right hand. He always kept it handy.

"How do you want to do this?"

"Follow me," he said and turned on his own flashlight.

Gary tucked the gun into his belt, at the back, hidden by his accessories vest.

They got out of the van and trailed after the man, who had already started down a rough dirt road worn through the woods.

If it had seemed dark at the roadside, it was nothing compared to the blackness among the trees that surrounded them.

The night bugs went silent as they walked along.

"How far is this place?" Gary said after walking for several minutes.

"We're almost there."

Soon they arrived at a break in the trees.

"Over here," the man said.

He took them to a spot where no grass was growing. There was a different kind of odor about it. None of the usual mosses and composting leaf smells one would expect in the woods.

Shining his light on nearby treetops, Gary could see the trees were dead.

"Some bad shit has been dumped here," their guide said.

He had a large zip bag and a garden trowel he used at the middle of the clearing to dig up a half-dozen small samples from different spots within a ten-foot circle.

Gary got a short video close-up of the man's hands as he collected the dirt and put each sample into the bag and zipped it shut.

"There's your proof." He handed the bag to Gary."

"Knowing what you know," Katt said. "Tucker would be running the risk of your reporting him."

"The arrogant bastard said something could happen to my family if I didn't keep my mouth shut."

"If what you say is true, that's still possible."

"No, they're in a safe place now. He can't get to them. But he knows where I am."

"Why did you come forward?" Gary said.

"Guilt for what I've already done. I don't want people to get hurt."

"Why now?" Katt said.

"When it was the woods, it was different. It was eating my guts, but I could almost live with it. Now that people are going to be living here and drinking water from wells dug on the property and their kids playing in crap that could ruin their health, it was time. Beyond time. I'm not proud of myself, but there it is."

"Why did you keep doing it if you felt so bad?"

"I just got out of the service and needed that job to support my family. I don't have a trade. The military is all I know. Didn't have a lot of choices that paid as well. When I saw your story on TV I decided I had to do something."

"Okay, now what?"

"Get the soil tested. I wouldn't know what to do after that."

Gary said, "We can cite an 'unnamed source,' but we really need some assurances that you will be there to back us up. If we report all this and you wimp out on us, we're in a lot of trouble."

"I will if you get some subcontractors with a beef and they are willing to talk on the record."

"How about if we interview you and not show your face," Katt said. "We can alter your voice and not give details that can identify you."

"That could work. I'd have to have some guarantee it wouldn't get out. I have two young daughters to think about."

Before they parted they agreed to meet at Gary's apartment the next evening for the interview.

"We never got the guy's name," Katt said.

"He wouldn't have given it to us if we'd asked."

<u>SEVEN</u>

When they arrived at the TV station the next morning, Katt and Gary filled Jerry in on what they had learned the night before.

"I dropped the soil sample off at a lab," Gary said.

"Gus couldn't reach you so he called me on the station land line," Jerry said.

Gary had turned the ringer off on his cell phone when he was out in the woods and had forgotten to turn it back on.

"He emailed a list of companies Tucker owned," Jerry said. "A bunch of separate corporations."

Jerry passed the list to Gary.

"Never heard of some of these." Gary picked up his phone. "I'm calling Gus back to see if he got anything else."

"Gary, I was just gonna call. You ESPeed on me, man."

"I'm looking at the list. Any idea what these companies do?"

"All kinds of businesses: Heavy equipment rental, apartment and office rentals, strip malls, waste removal—"

"Whoa! Waste removal. Our informant says Tucker has been dumping hazardous chemicals in that tract he wants to build on. Do you know what kinds of waste?"

"Universal Disposal, Incorporated lists chemicals—"

"That's it! Tucker's company has been collecting wastes. Instead of paying a legitimate outfit to process the stuff as the law requires, Tucker's stooge has been falsifying the paperwork to save money. Then someone like our guy carried the goop out there and dumped it."

"Go get 'em kimo sabe."

"Thanks. Gus," Gary said. "You always come through."

Later that afternoon Gary got a call.

"Mr. Mansfield, this is Michael Stokes at Allied Laboratory. I have your test results."

"I appreciate the fast service. What did you find?"

"The sample you provided showed a deadly concoction. Just about everything you would not want in your soil is present. I have rarely seen such a mixture of potentially lethal chemicals. A number of carcinogens."

Would you email me the list with any comments?"

Gary gave Stokes the email address and he could hear the clicking of a keyboard.

"It is in cyberspace as we speak, comments included."

Gary's cell phone pinged.

"Got it, thanks."

Gary forwarded the email to the editing room computer so he could print it.

Looking over the list, some of the chemicals were more common: formaldehyde, PCBs, pesticides, mercury. Others were unfamiliar.

"Christ!" Katt said. "Just the ones I know about can cause cancer."

Gary added the list to the growing collection of evidence.

The whistleblower called and set up an appointment for that evening.

Since Jerry had missed out on their trip through the woods, he joined Gary and Katt at their apartment

When the informant arrived they noticed that he looked completely worn out, as though he was seriously in need of sleep.

"You absolutely promise I can't be identified?"

Gary said, "We'll have you in silhouette and your own mother wouldn't recognize your voice."

A white background that lowered like a window shade was one of several blinds of various colors that were a permanent fixture along a wall in the apartment. The video camera was on a tripod. Lights were attached to the ceiling and on stands, but few of them would be used this night. A strong spotlight shown on the background and none on the subject, who was seated on a stool. He appeared in the camera as a shadow. Gary applied a false nose and chin somewhat larger than the man's own and a wig to make identifying him even more difficult. His voice would be unrecognizable.

"You sure no one will be able to identify me from this?"

"You won't look or sound like you," Gary said. "You have to be careful not to use a word or phrase or some reference that could only come from you. For our part, you're safe. We can't guarantee that Tucker can't find out in other ways."

The man thought about it for a moment. Then he said, "To hell with it. Let's do it."

With the camera rolling, Jerry said, "You say the Sierra Estates development proposed by the Tucker company is polluted land?"

"It's a toxic waste dump. I wouldn't be surprised if the feds listed it as a superfund site if they knew about it."

"What kind of wastes?"

"You name it. If it's bad for human health, it's in there. Formaldehyde; cyanide, mercury, all kinds of petroleum products—some with chemical names I can't even pronounce."

The man was clearly afraid. He was sweating liberally. By the time the interview was finished his shirt was soaked.

"You said Tucker kills people," Gary said as he removed the wig and fake nose. "What did you mean by that?"

"Some people who worked for him disappeared. Nothing to prove Tucker had anything to do with it, or even that they're dead, but it happened a few other times. Too much of a coincidence."

He gave them several names of the "disappeared."

"There may be more that I don't know about."

Gary asked for and received a contact number to reach him if necessary. He was still reluctant to give his name.

As he was preparing to leave, Gary gave a final assurance. "If anyone discovers your identity, you can be sure it didn't come from us."

The man nodded and left the apartment.

Katt was the first to speak. "If even half of what he said could be proved, Alex Tucker would go to prison. There would be millions of dollars of fines and cleanup costs."

But they knew that getting evidence against a wealthy man who appeared to be a respected member of the community would not be easy.

<u>EIGHT</u>

Team Jerry made short work of a fluffy feature story, their first assignment of the day. Then they headed to the disposal company. The business was located in the city's warehouse district. But when they arrived, they found a small storefront. It was locked.

"What kind of disposal business is this small and closed?" Gary said.

They looked through a window that was so filthy they could barely see inside.

"And what kind of business doesn't have any furniture?" Katt said.

A hand-printed sign with an emergency phone number was taped to the inside of the glass door.

"Well," Jerry said, "this is kind of an emergency?"

Gary set his cell phone so his number would not show up in the phone of the person at the other end. He dialed the disposal company. The call was answered on the second ring.

"Universal Disposal, This is Cheryl."

"This is Gary Mansfield from Channel Seven News. I wondered if I might stop by and talk to you."

There was a long pause.

"What is this about?"

"I can explain when we see you. The Universal Disposal office was closed. Where are you located?"

"I work out of my home. I guess it would be okay."

The woman gave Gary the address and agreed to meet them within the hour.

"That's interesting," Katt said. "I would have thought we would get a hard time and they'd refuse to talk to us."

Twenty minutes later they were parked in front of a modest ranch style home in a pleasant neighborhood.

"Weird place for a hazardous waste disposal company," Jerry said.

To their surprise, there was a ramp from street level with a switchback to the front stoop, making it easy for Jerry to navigate his wheelchair.

To their further surprise, the young woman in her mid twenties who answered the door was also in a wheelchair. She wore a full-length dress, no jewelry, and no makeup; a stunning natural beauty with a kind of gentleness about her. She looked at the trio with some suspicion, but motioned for them to come in.

It was not hard to tell that Jerry had a serious reaction to both the lovely lady and circumstances similar to his own.

"Cheryl Whistler," she said, extending a hand to each. "Jerry Harper, I see you all the time on the news. I feel as though I already know you. Please, come in and have a seat."

Jerry could not take his eyes off her as she guided them in.

She escorted them into the sparsely-decorated living room. Wall hangings consisted of photos; presumably family. One frame included a blue ribbon and a high school picture of a younger Cheryl Whistler. The ribbon said "First Prize Women's High Hurdles."

They were shown seating. Jerry, of course, had brought his chair with him.

"You have a very nice, neat home, Ms Whistler," Jerry said.

"Thank you. Please call me Cheryl."

"And please call me Jerry, Cheryl."

"I grew up in this house. Dad died three years ago. My mother passed away last year and I inherited the house. So I've never left home." She had a lovely, soft laugh.

"Something we have in common," Jerry said. "I also live with my parents, although I'm working at changing that."

Katt signaled covertly to Gary and Jerry to look at what would normally be a dining room that was set up as an office. Three telephones sat on a desk, each with more than a single line. Odd for home use.

"Now, how may I help you?"

Gary spoke first. "Ms Whistler—Cheryl—your company handles hazardous waste materials, is that right?"

"Let me stop you right there. First of all, it's not my company."

"How's that?"

"No, I just answer the phone. Universal Disposal is one of my clients. As you can see, like Jerry, my movements are rather limited. So are my employment opportunities. I act as a representative—a receptionist, if you will—for a number of companies that either can't afford a full-time employee or, in some cases, don't have an office, but want to appear to have one. Some of my clients work from their homes as I do, but their customers might not see a company with no brick and mortar location as a legitimate or capable business. Some small firms use mail drops as their address. That and a fancy letterhead, business cards, and me to answer their phone makes them look as big as the biggest companies. A harmless deception, I think, if the small company can do as good a job as the big one."

"I see your point," Jerry said.

"Now let me ask you a question," Cheryl said. "What is News Seven's interest in Universal Disposal?"

Gary hesitated just a beat to consider how much to tell her. He decided not to mention Alex Tucker.

"We have some concerns about some of their business practices," Gary said. We're looking into it."

"I hope I don't get in trouble with them by answering your questions."

"No way you would," Jerry said. "We won't say anything to anyone."

"I would hate to get them upset with me. I have eight clients, but losing even one would be a serious loss of income."

"Who owns Universal Disposal?" Jerry said, knowing very well who the owner was.

"I have no idea. My direct deposit pay lists only UD, Inc."

"But you must have some contact with the owners."

"Strictly by email. Both directions; sending and receiving."

"Didn't you think that was strange?" Jerry said, with the biggest smile Katt and Gary had ever seen on their young teammate.

Gary and Katt looked at each other. It was obvious there was a spark of interest between Cheryl and Jerry.

"Well," she continued with a smile equal to Jerry's. "It's different from how I communicate with my other clients."

"Didn't that seem a little odd?"

"I never thought of it is suspicious in any way. I speak to the other clients directly. But that's the way Universal wanted it and I simply comply. When a customer calls I tell them I will have the dispatcher get back to them to arrange a time for pickup. That is my total involvement in the transaction."

"So you don't really know who you work for beyond a ghost at the other end of an email."

"I don't question my clients' requirements. I simply do as they ask and continue to enjoy having a job. If I sensed anything was improper or illegal I would refuse their business. So far I have not had any reason to suspect anything out of the ordinary."

Other than the obviously intelligent young woman's limited mobility, she seemed in good health. Similar to Jerry's own situation she had assessed her limitations, considered her options, and made the necessary adjustments in her life and her means of making a living.

They got her personal phone number, gave her a business card with all three of their cell phone numbers, thanked her, and said their goodbyes.

Katt and Gary noticed that Jerry held onto Cheryl's hand longer than a simple goodbye handshake. She didn't seem in a hurry to let go of his hand either.

Back in the van, Katt said, "Is our little Jerry smitten?" She reached over and pinched his cheek which had turned very red.

"She is nice, isn't she?" Katt said. "Next thing you know you'll be coming your hair and brushing your teeth every day."

"Go for it, buddy," Gary said.

Jerry just smiled.

"We know Tucker owns Universal Disposal," Gary said as they drove back to the station. "He separates himself from discovery with another level of secrecy by having Cheryl act as the middle man . . . woman. Whoever acts as the dispatcher arranges for disposal."

"Universal is a separate corporation from Tucker's main enterprises," Katt said.

Gary nodded. "That way, if it all goes sideways he can separate any liability from his major interests. He would have other companies structured the same way for the same reason."

"I feel kinda bad for Cheryl," Jerry said.

"Why?" Katt said. "She isn't part of this."

"No, but if we put Tucker out of business, the poor girl is out of one-eighth of her living."

"Huh." Gary said. "I hadn't thought about that."

"We should find some more clients for her," Jerry said.

As they drove away, the team had not noticed there was a car parked at the end of the street with two large men inside.

<u>NINE</u>

When they returned to the station they were given two assignments that took them away from what Team Jerry really wanted to do. They finished them quickly.

When they were all finally back at the station and in their editing booth, Katt was frustrated and angry. "Stan does this on purpose, you know. He invents work so we won't do any investigating."

Gary reached over, put a hand on each of her cheeks and gave her a soft kiss.

She put her hands on her hips and looked up at him.

"That's your answer to everything, Gary. I get a good head of steam going and you kiss me. It was a very nice kiss, by the way."

"More where that came from."

Gary's cell phone rang. The caller was not identified.

"Mansfield."

"Mr. Mansfield, this is Officer Dale Collins of the Carsonville Police Department."

"Yes, officer, what can I do for you?"

"I am at Carsonville General Hospital with a Ms Cheryl Whistler."

"We know Cheryl. What's she doing at the hospital?" He put the phone on speaker.

Jerry in particular alerted.

"Ms Whistler has been injured."

"Dear God. How? What happened? Is she all right?"

Jerry spun his chair closer to the phone.

"She is not badly hurt and we have asked her what happened. She says she fell in her home. The staff thought she might be a domestic abuse case and reported it as the law requires. Ms Whistler has not admitted to any abuse. We're pretty sure she was beaten."

"She lives alone. Why do you think it was a beating?"

"Her injuries are not consistent with a fall. Multiple bruises and a mild concussion. She is sticking to her story and I wondered if you might have some idea of what happened?"

"Why me?"

"I found your business card in her jacket pocket and thought you might have had some contact with Ms Whistler that could lead us to whoever did this to her."

Gary, Katt, and Jerry exchanged looks, each having a pretty good idea of what happened. But they were not ready to open that can of worms.

"Sorry officer Collins. I talked to Ms Whistler earlier today on behalf of a friend who might want to use her answering services. I gave her my card. Is she going to be all right?"

"Oh, yes. No permanent damage. Looks like she was hit in the face and the ribs. Nothing serious. Unless she tells us otherwise we'll send her home. She's just here for observation. She will be leaving here within the hour."

"Sorry I can't be of any help, officer. She seems like a nice person."

"Thanks for your time."

"Shit, shit, shit!" Katt spat out.

Jerry was in a rage. "Somebody followed us. I never gave that possibility a thought. Damn me!"

"But how would they have gotten onto us?"Gary said.

"The only thing I can think of is that one of the subcontractors we talked to called Tucker to cover his own ass and Tucker put a tail on us."

"We can't go over there," Katt said. "Those guys could still be watching."

"I'll call her when I know she's back home," Gary said.

But Gary did not have to call Cheryl because Cheryl called him.

"Mr. Mansfield, this is Cheryl Whistler. You said you wouldn't tell anyone you talked to me."

"And I didn't," Gary said, putting the call on the speaker. "The only thing we can figure is that someone suspected we were investigating Universal Disposal and followed us to your place. I am so sorry this happened. Are you going to be all right?"

"I'll be fine. I've been hurt worse than this in real falls. They mostly slapped me hard in the face and a few punches in the ribs. I was afraid there might be some internal damage that I wouldn't be able to detect, so I went to the hospital. I'm still sore and plenty scared, but I'm all right."

"What did the people look like who did this to you?"

"Two big men. Muscular. They looked like what you would expect to see in the military."

Gary looked at Katt, who made a slashing motion across her throat. Gary knew very well who she had in mind as the slashee.

Jerry was way beyond livid.

"What did they want?" Jerry said.

"To know what you asked me and what I told them."

"What did you say?"

"Everything we talked about. That you suspected the owner of Universal Disposal of possible improper business practices, and that you were looking into it."

"But why did they beat you?"

"They didn't believe me when I told them I couldn't tell you anything about the disposal business because I didn't even know who owns it. My only contact is emails back and forth."

"Besides beating you up, how did they leave it?"

"They said if anyone asks, I should say I fell. If I said any more than that they would be back."

"The cop from the hospital said you stuck to that story, although they didn't believe it."

"What should I do?"

"Nothing. Just go about your work as always. I'm sure it's over. Just to be on the safe side I'm going to ask a friend on the police department to have officers drive by regularly to keep an eye on your place."

"I appreciate it. Would you do me a big favor?"

"Of course."

"If you learn more, please don't tell me. I don't want to know. I'm safer if I don't know anything."

"You're probably right."

When Gary hung up he called Carsonville Police Detective Lou Wagner.

"Lou, Gary."

"Okay, what kind of trouble are you in this time?"

Wagner had been Gary's partner when he was a cop. It had been five years since he quit the force.

"I'm not in any trouble," Gary said. "How can you even think that?"

"I think that because you are always in trouble."

"Well, not this time."

"That's a relief."

"However—"

"Oh, sh—here it comes."

"Someone in my recent acquaintance is in trouble."

Gary gave a sketchy version of the situation with Cheryl Whistler and some of the background as to the reason Cheryl was attacked.

"Who are you investigating?"

'That's not important, Lou. What is important is that we keep this young woman safe until we know there is no longer any danger."

Gary gave Lou Cheryl's address and was assured a patrol car would cruise by occasionally for a wellness check.

"You're investigating another bigwig, aren't you? It can't be the Russians because you wiped out all but one of them and he's in prison for life. Okay, who is it this time?"

One of the problems dealing with a top-notch detective, especially one Gary worked so closely with for so long, was that the man could practically read his mind.

"We need to talk, but not on the phone. Let's meet for lunch and I'll explain everything."

"All right, but you're buying."

"Okay you cheap bastard. Meet you at Lovies Diner at noon."

"Oh no. Lovies is where we go when I'm paying. I'll meet you at Arabesque at noon."

Arabesque was the most expensive restaurant in the city.

"You are a cruel man, Lou. Do you know that?"

"Hell yes. See you, sucker."

When he hung up, Gary called the Whistleblower, who picked up on the first ring.

"Hey, it's Gary."

"Any progress?"

"I wouldn't call it progress, but a small ray of enlightenment."

"I don't know what that means, but your call must mean something is going on."

Gary wasn't sure how to approach the subject, so he figured all he could do was jump right in.

"A woman we had been talking with was beaten today."

"Oh shit!"

"We aren't sure how they got onto us. We think we may have been followed to her home. I wanted to let you know so you can be alert for the possibility."

"I've been looking over my shoulder practically since I quit dumping that shit. Nothing new there."

"Do you have a weapon?"

"I have a Glock 17 and a carry permit."

Gary also had a concealed weapon permit. When he quit the police force he applied for his private investigator ticket, just to have another backup occupation.

"You served in the military, right?"

"Navy Seal."

"I'd say that should qualify you. Keep it handy."

"I don't advertise I'm armed. I want it to come as a surprise."

"I don't have any real reason to suspect that Tucker and company made a connection between us and you, but we can't be too careful."

The man was quiet for a moment.

"You still there?"

"Yeah. I gotta tell you something I hadn't told you before."

"What's that?"

"It's not only that I'm afraid of Tucker's thugs killing me."

"What else?"

"Sure, I'm feeling guilty about what I've done; yes I'm afraid of what those chemicals could do to residents of a development out there—especially kids—but there's another reason.

There was a long pause before he spoke again.

"I've got prostate cancer.

"Aw, man—"

"Don't know how far along it is. I don't have any health insurance. I didn't stay in the service long enough to retire, so I don't have a pension or VA medical. The cancer will only get worse and there's nothing I can do about it. Chances are I won't survive it without treatment. If Tucker's mugs don't get me first."

"Give me your home address. I'll get some police eyes on you. I'm sorry about this, man. We'll do everything we can to help."

"Appreciate it, Thanks for the warning." He gave them his address and hung up.

"Well, that sucks," Jerry said.

Gary thought back over the time between when the team spoke with contractors who had done business with Alex Tucker and when he and Katt accompanied their source into the polluted woods. Then the interview at their apartment. The visit to Gus's place. Were they being followed then?

Gary called Gus.

"Yo, Gary."

"Hey, buddy. Sooooo, how're things?"

"Things are—why do you ask like that? Has something happened?"

"Nothing. Not for sure and not yet."

"Ah, man. Is this where you tell me some mobster is gonna show up to kill my ass?"

"No, this is where I tell you if two large thugs show up on your surveillance video at your secret door and want to come in, you shouldn't let them."

Gus had hidden cameras all around the entrance to his place and a steel door equal in strength to a bank vault.

"I knew this was gonna happen. I told you—you said—"

"Don't panic. It's just that we think a couple of Tucker's thugs have been following us. We're just not sure whether they followed us to your place and I wanted to warn you."

"If I flip a coin 100 times it will come up 99 times the opposite of what I call. What are the odds that two shooters are gonna show up outside my door? I knew I should have said no to this, man."

"Nothing has happened. Just suggesting a little caution until we put Tucker out of business."

"There is not enough Dos Equis in the world that's worth getting murdered."

"Then I don't have to bother sending over those cases of beer?"

"Hold on. Let's not get radical, man. I'll keep an eye out and I'll let you know if they show."

Gary couldn't imagine that Tucker's men followed them into the woods. Too early in the game. But, after Cheryl Whistler's experience, he could not be sure about his apartment once they had started to talk to Alex's bilked subcontractors. If that were the case, Tucker and his crew might be onto the whistleblower. Gary decided to mention that to Lou at lunch.

Lou Wagner was waiting at the posh restaurant when Gary arrived.

"Anxious to spend my hard-earned money are you, Lou?"

"It's one of my few pleasures in life. Lunch at your expense and, of course, our weekly poker game, which I regard as my second income. How ya doin', buddy?"

Despite all the ribbing between them, Gary and Lou were the best of friends. Police partners often become closer than brothers because they depend on each other for their lives. Gary and Lou had been in those kinds of situations more than once when they worked together.

They had to wait a few minutes for a table.

"You were a hell of a cop, Gary," Lou said. "Nobody ever had a closing rate like you, before or since."

"We did it together, buddy. Don't give me all the credit."

"It was like you had some sixth sense. Remember that time we were tracking that whacko who shot up the auto parts store where he got fired?"

"Yeah. Killed his boss and another guy and injured two others."

"You predicted he would go to his mother's house. And he did. How did you know that?"

"I thought he realized he was in trouble and would go someplace he felt safe. Soldiers who get wounded in combat often cry out for their mothers. I figured she would be his comfort zone."

"I would never have thought of that. You did. Too bad the guy decided to shoot it out."

"If you remember, Lou, when we got back to the station the captain gave me shit for shooting the guy. The guy's mother said I should have shot the gun out of his hand the way they do in the movies. The captain sided with her. He didn't take it well when I challenged him to go to the range and shoot a gun-sized target out of the hand of a dummy."

"That captain isn't there anymore," Lou said. "I think the brass decided he wasn't a people person."

"The next one wouldn't have been any better. The position requires a person who kisses brass ass. He would be replaced with someone just like him. His type was the very reason I quit the force. The only thing I regret about leaving was not working with you anymore."

"You have it in your bones, Gary. Even in your TV job you can't help yourself. You still end up playing cop, which both pisses me off and scares the hell outta me.

When they were seated, Wagner said, "Paying for lunch. You must be in big trouble this time."

"Not me. Well, maybe."

Gary explained about the whistleblower and the answering service girl who acted as a receptionist for several work-at-home companies including one owned by Alex Tucker.

Gary didn't have to wait very long for an eruption from his friend.

"Alex Tucker! You lunatic! You couldn't take on a Mom and Pop convenience store for watering down the coffee. No, you had to go up against Mr. Moneybags. Are you nuts? Plus, you're playing cop again and I don't need to remind you, you are not a cop.

"If you're done," Gary said, "I will continue."

"I'm done for now, but you can expect some more reminders about your not being a cop."

"Let the record show that I am not a cop and I am well aware of it and need no further reminders."

Gary filled Lou in on most of what they knew and everything they suspected.

"So, you think Tucker's taking environmental shortcuts."

"I don't *think* it, Lou. I absolutely know it. The soil test shows it's a regular witch's brew out in those woods. Tucker is planning to dig wells and build right on top of it."

"Don't you think environmental impact studies would catch that?"

"Don't you get it?" Gary said, lowering his voice. "Alex Tucker has every agency in his pocket. The ones he can't buy, he threatens in other ways. He sics his personal two-man army on them. The rich always get their way, Lou. And he has the blessing of the state, county, and city because he brings money into the public treasuries. Not to mention political contributions."

"All that's beyond my control, pal."

"Yes, but you can provide some protection for the people who are helping us out."

Wagner sighed deeply. "What's your news director got to say about all this?"

"Exactly what you think he has to say about all this. And he doesn't even know about *all* of this."

"You know, Gary, one day you're gonna get yourself killed. Or worse, fired."

"If Stan "The Wuss" Hawkins tried to fire us I would make him a pariah in this town and in the next town he tried to get a job in. And he knows it."

"Okay," Wagner said, "I'll see what I can do. I'll alert some patrol guys I trust to keep an eye on both places."

Gary gave Lou the whistleblower's address.

"For this I'm ordering the filet mignon," Lou said.

Gary rolled his eyes and said, "I'll just have a salad."

<u>TEN</u>

Jerry called Cheryl Whistler that evening to tell her about the arrangement with the police. At least that is what he said he was calling about.

"Thank you, Jerry. I feel a little safer now."

"They don't really have any reason to come back, Cheryl. Even those two muscle-heads can figure out that you don't have any direct connection to Universal Disposal."

"Better to be safe, though."

"Yeah . . . uh . . . and . . ." Jerry was pausing a lot, having a little trouble getting around to the real reason he called.

"Was there something else, Jerry?"

"Uh . . . actually, yes. Cheryl. If . . . uh . . . if you are not otherwise involved, I wondered if you might want to go out to dinner with me sometime."

Cheryl got very quiet.

Jerry had a moment of panic, afraid he may have offended her or stumbled into forbidden territory. He broke the uncomfortable silence. "I mean, if you can't or don't want to, I'll understand."

"No, no. It's not that. It's just that no one has asked me out in a very long time."

"I can't imagine that. You're pretty—no, you're way beyond pretty, you're beautiful, you're smart, and you have your head on straight. I think we have a lot in common. Look, I like you, Cheryl. I don't know the whole you yet, but I'd like to get to know the rest of you."

"I have that sense about you, too, and I have a head start because I've watched you nearly every evening on TV. I don't think you can fake the warmth I see in your reports. So, no, I am not involved, and yes, I would like to go to dinner with you. But isn't there still that chance I'm being watched?"

"I doubt it. But to be sure, maybe we could meet somewhere. You drove yourself to the hospital, didn't you?"

"Yes, I have a mini-van with hand controls."

"Me too."

Each seemed reluctant to end the conversation. Every time either seemed to suggest the call was over, the other brought up something that kept it going. By the time they actually did end the call, more than an hour had passed.

"I work weekdays," Cheryl said. "I think I might be too tired to be good company."

"I can't imagine that you would ever be bad company, but okay, how about this Saturday?"

They agreed on a time and place the coming weekend.

When they finally hung up, Jerry thought his heart might burst through his chest.

ELEVEN

Assignments in hand, Team Jerry was out the door for another day of playing games with Stan Hawkins.

"I heard a rumor," Katt said on the way to the van.

"What?" Jerry said.

"That you and Cheryl are going out on a date."

Jerry stopped his wheelchair so suddenly the wheels skidded.

"How'd you hear about that?"

"Because I talked to Juliet personally, Romeo. I called last evening to see that she was okay and she said she talked to you. It took forever to get through because the line was tied up for a long time."

"Don't let Katt give you a hard time," Gary said. "Cheryl seems really nice."

"Okay," Katt said. "That's the last tease. I think she's one of those open people. What you see is what you get. Same as you, partner."

Jerry was unusually quiet as they drove to their first assignment. Finally he said, "It's not easy for me to meet girls that I would have any chance with. I'm sure women take one look and think there's no future for them with me; No kids, no full life. With Cheryl, we're in the same boat."

"But you don't like her just because she's also in a wheelchair," Katt said.

"That's the great thing. We do have that in common, but she's also a really nice person."

"She's the whole package, buddy," Gary said.

Team Jerry covered a multi-car freeway collision and a story about chickens being raised on an apartment building roof. Those stories were quickly gotten out of the way. The team huddled to talk about their assault on Alex Tucker's empire.

"We need someone on the inside," Jerry said.

"Good luck with that," Gary said.

Katt had an idea. "You remember that timid young girl at the press conference? The one who handed out news releases? I wonder if we could recruit her."

"As you say, she's timid. If she had any sense, she would be terrified of Tucker and those thugs he has doing his dirty work."

"Can't hurt to try."

"She'd respond to a woman easier than to a man," Jerry said. "Why don't you make a run at her? Maybe she has lunch in the restaurant on the ground floor of the Tucker building."

"I wouldn't want Tucker's people to see me with her," Katt said. "It'll have to be off-site."

Since it was nearly the time most employees have lunch, they headed to Tucker Tower.

They were wrong. The young woman did not have lunch in the downstairs restaurant. They spotted her leaving the building.

"I got her," Katt said. She opened the door of the van and stepped out to tail her.

"We have to consider that she will tell Tucker she was approached? Jerry said."

"Tucker already knows we're onto him," Katt said. "Nothing to lose."

She shut the door and was on the trail.

"Katt is really something," Jerry said. "She's the most fearless person I've ever known."

"You can have a lot of confidence when you know you can kill a man twice your size with your bare hands. I know because I've seen her do it."

"Whoa. That's a side of Katt I didn't know about."

"If you remember when I got into a gunfight with Russian mobsters who had kidnapped her, she jumped into the action and killed one of the gang with a single punch that crushed the man's windpipe."

"Well then, I'm especially glad we're friends."

Katt found it easy to keep up with someone on foot who had no reason to believe they were being followed. Still, she kept a reasonable distance behind her target.

The young woman turned down a tree-lined side street and went into a small café that was certainly a lot cheaper than the Tucker Tower restaurant.

Katt entered right behind her.

The place smelled of meals past mingled with meals present. Worn linoleum covered the floor except where old wood showed through. Fumes from the kitchen entered the dining room faster than exhaust fans could get rid of them. Katt knew her clothes would smell of grease and smoke for the rest of the day.

Alex Tucker wouldn't be caught dead in this joint.

The girl wore a plain pants outfit. No makeup, no jewelry, no adornments of any kind. It was as though she saw herself as plain and had convinced herself there was nothing she could do about it.

She found a seat at an unoccupied table.

Katt surprised her by sliding into a chair beside her.

"Ah. Do I know you?"

"Katt Li, I was at the news conference the other day."

"Yes, now I remember. You were one of the TV people."

"Look, Miss—"

"Simms. Alice Simms."

"Ms Simms. Let me make a very long story very short. Your boss is a criminal. No, that doesn't accurately describe him. He looks good; handsome, polished, smooth talker, but he's really a monster."

The young woman looked stunned.

"Please, you can't—"

"Here's the deal: The tract Tucker is proposing for Sierra Estates has been used as his hazardous waste dump for years. Despite that, he is going to develop it. The health of a lot of future residents is at stake."

"I really shouldn't be talking to you."

"You're right. You shouldn't. There would be some risk to you if you helped us prove what I just told you, so I won't spend a lot of time trying to convince you. All I will say is that if you do decide to help take down this wolf in sheep's clothing, no one will ever know about it from me."

Katt took out one of her business cards with her cell phone number written on the back and slid it across the table.

"If you decide to help, that's my personal number. I'm available day and night."

With that, Katt rose and left the restaurant, leaving the young woman looking confused.

She caught up with the van.

"That didn't take long," Jerry said. "She turn you down?"

"Won't know right away. I gave her the message. If she has a conscience and the courage we'll hear from her. If not, we'll hear from the goon squad."

"That's for sure anyway," Jerry said. "Had to try. What is that smell?"

"Eau de Greasy Spoon. It's all the rage."

Gary called Lou Wagner.

"Lou, Gary."

"I'm always surprised to learn you're not dead yet. What now?"

"We are moving forward. Maybe have an inside source. Don't know for sure yet.

"If Tucker is everything you say he is, you and anyone working with you will be targets."

"Well, you will know where to start looking if we turn up missing or dead."

"Since I can't stop you, the only thing Hank and I can do is help you. Not sure how we can do that, but it can't be official until there's some proof."

Detective Hank Reynolds was Lou Wagner's partner.

"As a matter of fact, you can do something. Tucker has two thugs doing his heavy lifting. If we can get pictures, could you run them though the system and get some information? They look like ex-military, maybe Special Ops types. Facial recognition should come up with something. You have that capability."

"I'd have to do it myself. I don't want this to leak."

"They stay close to Tucker unless he sends them out to kill subcontractors or beat up women. Should be easy to spot them. They look exactly like what you think they would look like."

"Watch your back, buddy." He hung up.

"That's a surprise," Katt said. "Lou and Hank always end up helping us, but you usually have to drag it out of Lou."

Gary knew his team and everyone associated with them were in danger. That Makarov handgun would be a regular fashion accessory from now on.

"Jerry, you shouldn't go to Cheryl's place."

"I already thought of that. We're meeting at a restaurant."

"Still, if they see you with her, she's back in their sights."

"We'll think of something."

"Jerry," Katt said. "I think you're in love."

"Maybe someday," Jerry said. "Right now I am seriously in like."

TWELVE

Gary was settling down in their apartment with Katt for the evening when his cell phone rang. The whistleblower's number came up on the screen.

"You okay?"

"I think I'm being followed."

"What makes you say that?" Gary said, putting the call on speaker.

"I see the same Dodge van a couple of cars back when I go anywhere. I'm at home now."

"You're sure it's the same van?"

"Pretty sure. I see two big silhouettes inside. I think it's more than my natural paranoia".

Katt was putting on a sweater.

"Let's assume it's Tucker's guys. You packing?"

"Always."

"Turn all but your essential lights off and stay away from windows. We'll be there in 15 minutes."

Gary hung up and called Lou as he and Katt raced out the door.

"What's up?"

"Our whistleblower thinks he's being followed. There's a good chance he's right."

"I'll call my patrol cops and have them swing by that neighborhood."

"Katt and I are on our way there now. Your guys should be looking for a Dodge van."

"I'd tell you to be careful, but I know you're not the type."

Katt and Gary made the short trip in record time.

"We should drive past the house first," Katt said. "Check out the neighborhood."

"Tucker's men will recognize this van. The patrol cops won't mistake our Chevy for a Dodge. Better check the alley, too."

Gary turned into the narrow passageway behind the whistleblower's house. A van was parked adjacent to the house. When the driver saw Gary's van, he started to pull away.

"They're speeding up," Katt said.

The van was almost to the street when a Carsonville Police patrol car pulled across in front of them, blocking their exit. They couldn't go forward and Gary had them trapped from the rear.

Katt and Gary got out and approached the van as the officers walked toward them.

Flashlight in one hand, the loaded and cocked Makarov in the other, Gary approached the driver's side.

"Friendly back here," he called out.

"Heard you were here," said one cop.

The officers approached cautiously, holsters unsnapped and their hands poised to draw. They were at a disadvantage walking into bright headlights.

Gary eased up to the driver's side and immediately identified the occupants as Tucker's men. He rapped the flashlight on the window, startling the driver.

"Turn off your headlights," Gary shouted.

The driver complied, but hesitated just long enough to assert his masculinity.

He rolled down his window just as the cop arrived.

"What's the problem, officer?"

"May I ask what is your business in this neighborhood?"

"Just out driving around. No law against that is there?"

While the cop had the attention of the two guys, Gary walked around in front of the van, raised his cell phone and took a picture of the surprised occupants before they had time to hide their faces.

They were the same two who brought the Sierra Estates diorama into the news conference.

Gary checked his photo file to be sure he got a good picture.

The cop walked to the rear of the van and was joined by Gary and Katt.

"He's right," the cop said quietly. "There is no law against driving around. We have to let them go."

"Hold off on that for just a minute officer—"

"—Brunner, Bob Brunner," he said. "Heard you used to be a cop."

"I left the job five years ago. Can't seem to get out of the habit. Hang on here, I'll be right back."

Gary walked through the back yard and called the whistleblower. He picked up on the first ring.

"You Okay?"

"Yeah, what's going on back there?"

"You were right, it's Tucker's men."

"Shit."

"Well, the good news is that we know they know. The better news is that we have placed them within 50-feet of your house. The police have a record of it and I took a picture of them."

"Yeah, I guess that's good news. Shows you that paranoia pays off sometimes. My week to have the kids is coming up. I'll tell the ex I can't do it. She'll be pissed, but she's always pissed at me anyway, so no great tragedy there."

"My phone is on 24/7. Call anytime. You might want to stack pots and pans on the floor inside your outside doors as a kind of early warning system."

"I guess it's the price of doing the right thing."

"You know, I never did get your name," Gary said.

"It's Manning. Lester Manning."

"Have a good evening, Lester," Gary said and rejoined the police.

"You can let them go, Bob," Gary said quietly. "My guy is okay."

Brunner went to the driver's side of the van and told them they could leave as soon as he moved the patrol car.

The driver shot a dirty look at Gary, which said a lot about what Gary might expect in the future.

Katt looked like she wanted to rip their hearts out. With her, that was more than just an expression.

When they were gone, Gary and Katt thanked the cops. "Now that we've placed them within shooting distance of the guy we're trying to protect, I doubt they'll try here again. To be on the safe side you should continue your occasional drive-by."

"That's the plan," Brunner said and drove away.

"That was refreshing," Katt said.

"It's looking more and more like our only option is to exterminate a couple of guys."

"Lou wouldn't like that, but you have my vote."

Gary called Lou again and started to fill him in on the adventure.

"I already got the story from Brunner."

"I'm sending you a picture of the two men for facial recognition. Maybe you can find something that could take them out of circulation."

"Nothing ever goes that easy, pal."

"I'm an optimist," Gary said. "You know that."

"And I'm one-eyed, one-horn flying purple people eater."

"Huh?" Gary said and hung up.

THIRTEEN

I guess I should take up praying," Jerry said when they briefed him at the TV station about the events of the previous evening.

"Or you could take up poker," Gary said. "Wednesdays are poker nights.

"Then I definitely should take up praying because I've never played poker."

"Then you definitely should join us," Gary said. "You'll learn in time."

"I don't think I can afford the lessons."

"We all have to pay for our education, Jerry."

"I have to be somewhere tonight."

"Where?"

"Give me a minute. I'll think of somewhere."

"Seven o'clock tonight," Gary said. "Our place."

"Who all will be there?"

"Just Katt and me, Lou Wagner, and his partner, Hank Reynolds."

Jerry raised his eyebrows. "You play, too, Katt?"

"Of course. Don't act so surprised. Girls play poker, too, you know."

Gary laughed, but stopped when Katt shot a dirty look at him.

"I'm not sure you can call what Katt does is *'playing'*," Gary said. "Katt turns into an entirely different person at poker. It's kind of frightening when you consider that her body is a lethal weapon."

Katt got a little pouty. "I'm the same as I always am when I play."

"Well," Jerry said, "that's pretty scary right there."

"Shut up."

Gary turned serious. "Jerry, we gotta get you armed."

"Oh, man, I'm not sure that's a good idea."

"You think those mercenaries are going to ask you politely not to investigate their boss?"

"I don't think I could shoot anyone."

"Picture this: you're sitting with your girlfriend and two hairy apes come at you with guns. You're armed with a smile and a positive attitude. Sweet talk may work with Cheryl, but what are the odds of it working with those guys?"

"I'm more likely to shoot the wrong person than to defend myself."

"I have a spare handgun that's perfect for you. I'll book us at the range Saturday morning for some basic firearms familiarity. Lou will attest to your need for protection so you can apply for a permit. We'll sign you up in a training program. Getting you permitted shouldn't be too hard."

Gary was the permanent host of the weekly poker party since none of the other participants had a place for it. Hank and Lou were married men, with wives who didn't want their homes to become gambling dens smelling of cigar smoke. That was fine with both of them because it was the perfect excuse to get out of the house.

A felt-topped card table was not the typical furnishing in most homes, but was standard equipment and a long-standing Wednesday night tradition at Gary's apartment.

Poker, beer, and cigars, the Holy Trinity.

Although none of them were smokers, the weekly cigars were the exception. The room was thick with smoke as five people were seated around the table instead of the usual four.

"A good thing we live on the ground floor, huh Jerry?" Gary said.

"Lucky me. Otherwise I couldn't be here to lose all my money."

"We needed some new blood," Lou Wagner said. "We've heard all these guys' stories. What's yours, Jerry?"

"Same as yours, but on wheels."

"I heard you got a girlfriend," Hank Reynolds said.

"She's not my girlfriend, she's a girl I met and like and we're going out Saturday night."

"Sounds like a girlfriend to me," Katt said, a cellophane-wrapped, unlit cigar sticking out of the corner of her mouth and a bottle of beer in one hand.

"Didn't your parents teach you to be kind to the handicapped," Jerry said.

"They did," Katt said. "Do you know any?"

Jerry looked at her like she just got in from Venus.

"Jerry is one of the most able people I've ever known," Katt said. "He just can't walk."

"That's sort of a handicap," Jerry said.

"More of an inconvenience in your case," Gary said. "When we got rid of the knucklehead who preceded Jerry as field reporter, he eased right into the job like he was made for it. When he was our intern he learned the job of everyone at the station except the engineers and juggled it all with a full college load."

"Interesting that you all don't shy away from talking about Jerry's situation," Hank said.

"We talk about everything," Jerry said. "No taboos with us. Want to know about catheters and colostomy bags?"

"Pass," Hank said. "But thanks anyway."

The mood was light, but everyone in the room was aware of the danger Team Jerry was facing since they started investigating Alex Tucker.

"I'm getting Jerry gunned up," Gary said.

That got Lou Wagner's attention.

"Normally I don't think civilians should carry guns," Wagner said. "Considering the current threat, it's a good idea. But only after some training and permitting."

"Starting this weekend," Gary said. "We'll need your endorsement."

"How about some poker," Hank said. "This being poker night and all."

"Okay, you deal."

Jerry looked at his cards as though they might bite him.

"Just remember what I taught you, Jer," Katt said.

"You taught him to play poker?" Lou said. "Aw, crap. What'd you go and do that for?"

Jerry smiled, took a drag on his cigar, coughed until his eyes watered, put it out in an ashtray, vowed never again, anted up, and won the first hand.

And the second, third, and most of the rest of them.

"I blame you, Katt," Lou said. "We had a perfectly good patsy lined up and you had to go and—"

Hank sat straight up in his chair. "I just heard glass breaking?"

Three guns came out at the same time. Everyone headed for the front door.

Gary pulled the door open and was greeted with a wall of flames.

Katt grabbed a fire extinguisher from the kitchen as the two detectives scanned the floodlighted parking lot for the arsonist who might be waiting for them to come out to be shot. Seeing no one, Katt continued to battle the blaze. Gary retrieved a second fire extinguisher from the pantry and joined Katt in the fight.

When the fire was completely extinguished, Gary said, "I guess we know who's responsible for this."

Gary looked over the charred front stoop area. "The fire did more damage to the paint than to the wood. We caught it in time. Still, we should keep an eye on it to make sure nothing flares up."

Katt continued to direct the fire extinguisher on the blackened surface.

"Those guys seriously need to be killed," said homicide detective Lou Wagner.

"I second the emotion," Hank Reynolds said.

"I am on record as a volunteer," Katt said.

"I'll tell the patrol guys to add your place to their list for extra attention," Lou said. "Your apartment is still vulnerable, even when you're not here. And there are seven connected units to consider. Burn one, you've burned them all."

Gary phoned Lester Manning.

"Our goons lobbed a Molotov cocktail at our apartment," Gary said. 'We caught it in time."

"I may have to go after those guys myself."

"Don't put yourself in danger,"

"What have I got to lose? I'm probably dead either way."

"You're too important to putting Tucker out of business to get yourself killed before you can testify. These guys are pros."

"If you remember, I'm kind of a pro myself."

Gary rejoined the party.

"Okay," Hank said. "Now that we got that little matter out of the way, could we play some poker?"

"Jerry has pretty much cleaned me out," Lou said.

"This was so much fun," Jerry said. "I can hardly wait until next week."

A chorus of groans.

The rest of the evening was spent in quiet conversation with cards left for another time.

"Still reluctant to carry a gun, Jerry?" Gary said.

"I'm warming up to the idea."

FOURTEEN

The rest of the week passed without incident. Jerry met up with Gary at the city shooting range Saturday morning.

Gary had brought his backup weapon, a .380 caliber Colt Mustang semi-automatic, and several boxes of ammunition, two extra magazines, and hearing protectors for both of them. He ran through the safety procedures, emphasizing the danger of handling a firearm.

The firing range had a dozen lanes with about half of them filled with shooters. Each lane had a table to use as a rest or as a place to lay out the ammo boxes. A hundred yards away was a twenty-foot-high dirt embankment that, after years of absorbing bullets that overshot the targets, the embankment no doubt held as much lead as dirt.

"We'll set the target at 25 yards. The goal is to get as many shots in the black as possible."

Gary explained how to grip the weapon with two hands, line the sight up with the center of the target, then slowly squeeze, rather than jerk, the trigger. He ran the target out on a track to the 25-yard mark.

Jerry did as instructed.

After one clip had been emptied, Gary pulled the target in to see the results. To say Gary was surprised would be an understatement.

"Jerry! You scored two dead center and the rest well in the black. That is amazing shooting. If you can hit something that small at 25 yards, you can hit a man's torso at ten feet, no problem.

They shot several more clips with similar results before packing up.

Jerry was learning to shoot a gun as quickly as he had learned the game of poker.

"Tonight's the big date," Gary said.

"We'll see if we still like each other at the end of the evening."

"I'd put my money on long term."

Jerry had thought Saturday night would never come. Now that it had, he was nervous. He had made it a regular habit lately to check to see if anyone was following him. He took a roundabout route to the restaurant where he was to meet Cheryl, but did not see any obvious signs he had a tail.

She was already waiting for him at a table at an out-of-the-way spot in the dining room. It had been set up for two diners in wheelchairs. They would not be in the way of foot traffic. They were in a location where they could talk without having to shout over kitchen clatter.

Cheryl was wearing a full-length dress and a lightweight sweater over a top that was slightly low-cut without being provocative. She wore a little lipstick in a light shade and no jewelry.

Jerry was awestruck. "You look beautiful."

Embarrassed, she said, "Thank you. You look quite handsome yourself."

Jerry had worn a brown suit that was too dark to wear on-camera.

"No unfriendly visits, I presume?"

"No. I'm sure you're right about their having no further interest in me."

Jerry had decided not to mention the firebombing. No point in alarming her.

"I meant to ask you how you got into the receptionist business."

"It's just an updated version of the old answering services that were popular before cell phone voice mail and email eliminated that niche."

"A brilliant idea. You found a need and filled it."

"I doubt that I invented the concept, but it seemed to me there might be a market and I was right.

Cheryl could have been reading the stock market report and Jerry would have been just as fascinated watching her.

They had been so involved in conversation that they had not even looked at the menu by the time the server stopped by. They requested a few more minutes.

"We should go Dutch," Cheryl said.

"No, no, this is my treat. And you don't have to read the right-hand column of the menu either. They pay me pretty well at the station. Except for my contribution to living with my parents, I don't have many places to spend it. The money just keeps piling up in my checking account. I want this to be a memorable evening for you."

"You've already made it that by inviting me. I haven't had a date since high school."

"Is that when—"

"Yes. My prom date was driving and we got hit in the passenger side by a drunk driver. I was pinned and I got the spine injury that put me in this chair."

"Pretty much what happened in my accident; drunk driver, pinned, spinal injury. It seems not everything we have in common is good."

The next time the server came by they were ready to order.

The food was good, but as far as Jerry was concerned it could have been Big Macs and fries because he barely noticed it. Just spending time with this sweet young woman was the real benefit. He decided on the spot that there would be as many more times like this as she would have him.

Both seemed reluctant for the evening to end. They agreed to get together at her home in a few days. Phone calls in-between.

They adjourned to the parking lot where they said good night a half dozen times, but continued to not leave.

"I would like to kiss you," Jerry said.

"And I would like for you to kiss me."

And so they did. Their very first kiss, right there in the restaurant parking lot.

They were so focused on each other they did not notice a van parked with a view of the restaurant lot. It seems one of them had been followed after all.

FIFTEEN

When Jerry arrived at the station Monday morning he still had the smile his evening with Cheryl had put there.

His teammates were lying in wait for him.

"How was the hot date," Gary said.

"We had a great time. She's even nicer than I thought."

"I guess you'll be seeing her again then," Katt said.

"Good guess."

Katt and Gary had decided not to tease Jerry as much. Their friend had found something to be happy about. Rare in the young man's life.

"So, team," Katt said, "what can we do today to make Mr. Tucker's life miserable?"

"The more I think about it," Gary said, "the more I think he should have an 'accident' and save a lot of trouble."

"Yeah, we could whack him in the head and leave a banana peel at the scene," Katt said. "I can see the headline: 'Carsonville Millionaire has fatal slip on banana peel.'"

"I like it," Jerry said. "The cops would never trace it to us because we don't bring our lunches. But just about every brown bagger in the city would be a suspect."

The light mood was interrupted when Jerry's cell phone rang. Cheryl's name came up on the screen.

"Good morning," Jerry said.

"Just listen, asshole."

Jerry's face registered absolute terror.

"Who is this? What have you done with Cheryl?"

Jerry flipped the phone on speaker as Gary and Katt gathered around.

"Nothing yet. But that could change if you don't back off what you've been doing."

"If you've hurt her, I'll—"

"We won't call again. You've been warned. It's up to you now,"

The caller hung up.

Jerry frantically hit Cheryl's number on speed dial. She picked up on the first ring.

"They're gone."

"Are you okay? Did they hurt you?"

"I'm okay. Shaken. All they did was use my cell phone to call you."

"How did they know?"

"They must have followed one of us Saturday night."

"I was really careful. I drove around the city for a half hour before I went to the restaurant."

"I'm scared, Jerry."

"Hang on. I'll be right there."

Jerry hung up and raced to the door.

Gary and Katt followed. "We're going with you."

Stan Hawkins saw them heading to the parking lot.

"Where are you guys going?" Hawkins said. "I didn't give you an assignment."

"We're taking a sick day, Stan." Katt said.

"All three of you at the same time?"

"Yeah," Gary said. "Must have been something we ate."

"Why don't I believe you?"

"You know, Stan," Gary said. "Sometimes I wonder why this isn't a union shop. Maybe we should look into that."

Hawkins spun around and went back to his desk so fast he might have gotten a whiplash.

Jerry was already in his mini-van. Katt jumped in the front seat with him, Gary in the back, next to the wheelchair, and they were on their way at barely legal speed.

In record time they screeched to a stop in front of Cheryl's house.

Katt and Gary ran to the house as Jerry struggled to get into his chair.

Cheryl met them at the door. She was shaking from fear.

"How could they know I was seeing Jerry?" Cheryl said.

"I'm afraid we have underestimated these guys," Gary said.

Jerry had joined them. "There is no way they followed me," he said. "I was really careful. And they had no reason to follow Cheryl."

Gary had a faraway look. Then he ran out the door to Jerry's van. He walked all around the vehicle, getting down on his hands and knees and looking at the underside. He seemed to be reaching for something. He got up and walked back to the house with a small object in his hand.

"A tracker," he said. "It's an electronic device to let them know where you are at all times. They didn't tail you, Jerry. They put the device on your van when it was parked. All they had to do was follow the little red dot on a screen. They must have seen you with Cheryl at the restaurant."

"Omigod," Cheryl said. "What am I going to do?"

"We have to get you to a safe place."

"I can't leave my customers. I'd lose them all if I'm not here to answer their calls."

Katt saw the dilemma and came up with a solution.

"I have an idea," Katt said. "Cheryl, would you mind if someone stayed here with you?"

"Who?"

"We have a friend who runs a security business. Ex-cop. But before that he was Army Special Forces. They could put an armed guard here around the clock."

"Pat Anderson got fed up with the police department around the same time I did," Gary said. "We've stayed in touch."

"I couldn't afford something like that."

"Don't worry about it," Katt said. "I'll take care of it."

"Oh, Katt. I couldn't let you do that."

Gary laughed. "There's no way you could know," he said, "but Katt is rich."

Both Cheryl's and Jerry's eyes went wide."

"Yeah," Katt said. "When the man died who adopted me after I escaped from foster care as a kid he willed me a load of money and property. I sold all the property and I've since made some good investments and parlayed that into a pretty hefty fortune."

"But it's your money, Katt."

"A drop in the bucket and I have nothing better to do with it. I almost forgot I had it. Even Jerry didn't know about it and we're as close as kin."

"If you can stand having an armed guard in your house with you until this is resolved," Gary said. "I'll call and get the ball rolling."

Cheryl nodded. "I don't know how I can ever repay you."

"Cheryl," Jerry said, "we got you into this mess and, while I've only known you for a short time, I know I don't want anything to happen to you. So, if you agree to a guard, it's as good as done."

Katt took that as a signal to leave. "We'll wait in the car," Katt said, and left them to talk

"We should check our own vehicles for trackers," Gary said.

When Jerry joined them, Gary was already on the phone to the security company to make arrangements for armed, on-site protection to begin immediately.

"Pat, Gary. Got some bodyguard business for you."

"Somebody after you, Gary?"

"No,. Well, sort of, but it's not for me, it's for a friend of ours."

"How soon and how heavy?" Pat Anderson said.

"Yesterday and the best, baddest, most aggressive, shoot-first-ask-questions-later people you have for round-the-clock duty."

"That pretty much describes my entire staff, including my secretary. Your friend must really be in big trouble."

"Not if your people are here to head it off. I should warn you; they could be going up against what we think are two well-trained ex-military types."

"I have just the right people and the best of the best will leave here as soon as you give me the address."

Gary could hear Anderson shouting in the background to gear up for heavy duty and be ready to hit the road.

Gary gave him the address. "We'll wait in front of the house until they get here.'

"I'll never be able to repay you for this, Katt," Jerry said.

"Damn right. You owe me. You can start repaying by always taking my side in any argument I have with Gary."

"Deal."

"Hey!"

"You've said it yourself, Gary. The rich always have their way."

"So, you're an heiress," Jerry said.

"Yep. Disgustingly rich. That's part of the reason it's so easy for me to tell Stan Hawkins to pound sand."

"You'd do it anyway," Gary said. "But what about me?"

"I will always take care of my wittle snookums."

"I think I may throw up," Jerry said.

A yellow van with "Anderson Security" in big letters on its sides came screeching around a corner and pulled up behind them.

A tall, robust woman dressed for combat stepped out.

When he got over his surprise, Gary got out to brief Anderson's "best-of-the-best." Her name was Janet Mohn. At over six feet tall, she weighed in the 200 pounds range, not counting the body armor she was wearing, and there was not enough fat on her six-foot-plus frame to fry an egg. Large, but beyond that, she was an enormous presence. This was one sturdy individual. She looked very much like she could take care of herself as well as whoever she was protecting.

"Two big thugs," Gary said. "Ex-military for sure. Well-trained killers, not to be underestimated. Shoot first because they certainly won't hesitate."

"Shoot first is my motto," Mohn said in a deep voice. "Should have it tattooed on my ass."

"I think if you leave the marked van at the curb they will come in better prepared. If they don't know there is security you may have the advantage."

"My thought exactly. If they don't know I'm here," she said, patting her sidearm. "Before they have a chance to draw their weapons I can give them 17 reasons why they should have stayed at home. I'll have one of our guys bring an unmarked and trade it for this one."

She made the call.

As they prepared to leave, Gary introduced Janet to Cheryl, who seemed relieved to see her and the Glock semi-automatic holstered on her hip and a Remington military shotgun slung over her shoulder.

That done, Jerry said a reluctant goodbye to Cheryl and the three of them got back into Jerry's van.

"That is one tough cookie," Gary said. "I would truly hate to have her mad at me."

"Short of hunting Tucker's guys down," Katt said, "we've done everything that can be done. Since we're taking a sick day anyway we may as well make good use of the time."

Gary agreed. "Jerry, I want you to keep the Mustang with you, I know you're not legal yet, but we can put your carry permit on the fast track. We'll get you signed up for the required training classes."

Gary called Lou.

"Our thugs threatened Jerry's girlfriend if we don't back off."

"Christ! Are those guys still alive?"

"Sadly, yes. But only because I don't know where they are at the moment. We put a 24/7 armed security guard on her

"Anderson's outfit, I hope."

"Yep."

"That oughta slow them down. Pat's the best. It was a sad day when he left the force."

"You find out anything about those two?"

"I was gonna call you. You were right about ex military. Joseph Carnahan, U.S. Army Ranger until four years ago when he punched out his company commander. Nearly killed the dude and earned him a dishonorable discharge."

"That figures. And the other guy?"

"Ex Ranger Melvin Gingrich. Same story, except it was a recruit he beat nearly to death. If the guy'd died our thug would be in Leavenworth."

"He should be there anyway. So he gets a dishonorable and promises to be kind to his mother."

"Guys like that were made in a lab. They don't have mothers."

<u>SIXTEEN</u>

After Team Jerry switched to Gary's van, Jerry called Cheryl.

"You okay?"

"Still scared, but it's some comfort to have Janet here."

"There's an end to this. I just can't say when. We are going to neutralize Tucker and his crew."

"You should be careful, too."

"I'm as well protected as you are. Gary and Katt are nobody to be messed with. I'll tell you about Katt sometime."

"Stay in touch. Call me lots."

When he hung up the phone, Katt tried to reassure him that Cheryl would be safe, although she was having a hard time convincing herself.

"We should get Gus involved," Gary said.

Katt called Gus and put him on speaker.

"Gus, Katt."

"Hola sweet thing. You finally decided to dump Gary and give me a shot?"

"No, I'm keeping him, but you're on my short list if I go looking for a replacement."

Gary laughed out loud.

"How may I serve you today my pint-size samurai?"

"Samurai is Japanese. I'm half Chinese. We have need of your services."

"Ah, man. Are you going to appeal to my sick need to live on the edge."

"Yes I am."

"Okay, I'm in. What do I do?"

"Why don't we swing by and kick around some ideas."

"See ya."

"We have turned that poor man into an adrenaline junkie."

"He's always been that way," Gary said as he turned the van toward Gus's place.

Gary and Katt had found trackers on their own vehicles, but left the magnetized devices stuck on metal light poles in the TV station parking lot when they went anywhere they didn't want Tucker's men to know about.

Gus welcomed them to his hideaway.

"You want me to help you to bring Mr. Tucker down."

"We do," Gary said. "Any and all methods fair and foul are on the table. This guy has to be put out of business."

"What are his weak spots?"

"His ego, for one," Katt said. "His money, for another."

"So, if I give him some money troubles, we shake him up. He's a guy who can't imagine not being in control."

"That about sums it up," Jerry said.

"Okay then, the trick is to take some of that control away from him, hit him in the wallet, and make him look like an idiot to the public. That should shake up his ego."

"And make him lash out," Gary said. "Which I admit comes with its own set of problems.

"And he'll do something stupid," Katt said. "Desperate people make mistakes."

"Full frontal assault," Gus said. "If he's like most rich people he has some off-shore accounts."

"True," Gary said. "To hide money from the tax man."

"I have one myself," Gus said.

"Me, too," Katt said. "But not to cheat the tax man. Only a couple hundred thousand dollars in it. Just thought it would be good to have one."

"*Only* a couple hundred thousand dollars?" Jerry said. "I never use the words 'only' and 'money' in the same sentence."

"I'll get right on it," Gus said. "By the way, am I doing this for the love of adventure alone?"

"No," Gary said, "You're doing it out of loyalty to a treasured friend—"

"What?

"And for a case of Mexico's finest Dos Equis beer."

"That's more like it. Anyone who gives me the Two Xs, I am their slave. I'll call when I have something."

"We'll all go out to dinner at a swell restaurant when this is over," Gary said.

"Assuming we survive."

Back at the TV station, Gary's phone rang. "It's Gus."
"Gimme good news."
"I was right about offshore accounts."
"Can you access them?"
"If I had some account numbers and passwords I could. I'll try to worm my way into his corporate computer system. Maybe they're in there."
"Can you do it?"
"Am I not The Shadow mi amigo?"
"That you are, amigo. Hop to it Shadowman."
Gary clicked off.
"I can't believe anyone would be stupid enough to write down account numbers and passwords where anyone could access them," Gary said. "But it's worth a try."
"If anyone could find them, it would be Gus," Katt said.
"I'm going to check with Cheryl," Jerry said, hitting speed dial.
"Hi, I'm glad you called."
"Why, has something happened?"
"No, I'm just glad you called."
"I can't tell you how nice it is to have someone who is glad to hear from me. You and Janet getting along okay?"
"I have full confidence in Janet's ability to handle evil-doers."
Jerry could hear laughter.
"We're getting along like we've known each other forever. I think we'll still be friends after this is over."
Jerry heard Janet shout, *"count on it, baby doll."*
"You do have that effect on people."
"What have you guys been doing?"
"Not good to talk specifics over the phone. But we have been productive."
"That's encouraging. I can't wait to hear about it when I see you. Soon, I hope."
"This evening, for sure."
"Good, I'll fix dinner for us here. Will there be the three of you or just the one of you?"

"Just me. I'll ditch these two."

"Hey," Katt said.

". . . and I'll see you around seven o'clock."

When Jerry hung up the phone, Gary reached under the driver's seat, fished out the Colt Mustang and handed it to Jerry with two extra loaded magazines.

"Now that you know how it works, you should hide it behind you on your chair where you could reach it quickly if you had to."

"I'm still a little hinky about the idea of shooting someone."

"You'll know what to do if the time comes. Better to have it and not need it than need it and not have it. There is a round in the chamber. All you have to do is flip the safety off, point and squeeze the trigger."

It had been a tiring day for Jerry. Living in a wheelchair is no easy job. Upper body strength develops incredibly. But all that lifting, tugging, and working the wheels wears a person out.

But he was rejuvenated as he arrived at Cheryl's.

Before he even got to the door he could smell something amazing coming from the house.

"Don't shoot, it's just me."

Jerry entered the living room and was slightly startled to see a very large man wearing combat gear standing next to Cheryl.

"Where's Janet?

"Shift change," Cheryl said. "She's off duty. She was reluctant to leave. This is Luke. Luke, Jerry."

He nodded and shook Jerry's hand. It was plain to see that Luke was a man of few—if any—words.

"I made lasagna. I hope you like Italian."

"I do. And several other nationalities," he said.

Cheryl giggled.

They adjourned to a nook in the kitchen. The seat on one side of the table had been removed and the space widened to accommodate Cheryl's wheelchair. Jerry's place was at the end of the table, which suited him just fine because it put him closer to Cheryl.

"No formal dining room? How primitive."

"I had a choice; a dining room or an office."

"Won't Luke be joining us?"

"No, he said he can't do anything to take his attention away from what could be coming through the front door." The back door had already been barricaded.

The table was already set. Cheryl opened the oven door, took out the lasagna, and sliced it into serving-sized segments and fixed Jerry a plate.

"You made this?"

"I did."

"Smart, beautiful—and she cooks. Gary said you were the whole package and this proves it."

"How nice of Gary. He and Katt are a couple, aren't they?"

"You could tell that, huh? It took them a few years of working together to realize they were meant for each other. And they are the best friends I have ever had."

As they were finishing the meal, Luke looked into the kitchen.

"A Dodge van just drove by real slow," he said. "You should stay back here until I figure out if it's our bogies."

An hour passed before Luke declared it safe.

"Maybe nothing. Could be someone looking for a house number. At worst it was the bad guys who saw three vehicles parked out in front and the whole house lit up. Maybe figured they'd come back when there were fewer people around."

It took awhile for Jerry to be convinced that he didn't have to stay, that Luke and a backup guy he called in for the occasion could handle anything that came up.

With double the protection, Jerry and Cheryl enjoyed their second kiss before he left for home.

<u>SEVENTEEN</u>

Katt and Gary had just arrived at their apartment when Katt's cell phone rang. She didn't recognize the caller's number.

"Katt here."

"Ms Li, this is Alice Simms. We met at—"

"Yes, yes Ms Simms." Katt put the call on speaker. "Have you thought about what I said?"

"I have thought of nothing else since then."

"And your conclusion?"

"I have decided to help you, but I'm really scared."

"You should be. We're talking about a dangerous man. I don't want to minimize the danger."

"I understand. What can I do?"

"We should discuss it in-person, but we have to be sure Tucker's men don't follow us."

"They are usually in the office with him. I could meet you at lunch time when I know where they are. I always leave at noon so there would be no reason for them to suspect anything."

"Perfect. How about tomorrow at that same restaurant where we met?"

Katt heard the nervousness in her voice.

"Okay. I will see you there tomorrow. Bye."

Gary said, "We have to take extra precautions so they don't find out Alice is working with us."

"The restaurant meeting should be safe enough, but after that we're going to have to get creative in how we exchange information. Never face-to-face."

Katt was on her third cup of mint tea when Alice Simms came through the door of the restaurant. Katt made sure to arrive well ahead of Alex Tucker's intern so it would not look as though they got there together.

Katt would not have been surprised if the young woman had changed her mind about helping to get incriminating evidence against her boss. Tucker was a vindictive man. She would be doing it at great risk to herself.

Alice saw Katt, who was seated in a booth that was not visible through the street-side windows.

It was obvious from clear across the dining room that Alice was a nervous wreck.

Katt thought it was unlikely that Tucker had reason to suspect that she was working against his interests and had her followed. That is, unless he got curious about why she was looking so jittery.

Alice slid into a chair opposite Katt with her back to the dining room.

"I'm surprised you came," Katt said.

"I almost didn't. I'm so scared."

The waitress came to the table and Alice ordered a hot chocolate and a BLT.

"What made you decide to show up?" Katt said.

"After you told me Mr. Tucker was a criminal I remembered a couple of things and I started looking at him differently. Before that I just did what the office staff asked me to do. I make copies, refill or un-jam the copy machine, file documents, run errands, that kind of thing. The longer I was there, the more they didn't seem to really notice me. I think I'm becoming kind of invisible around there."

"What made you suspicious?"

"I guess I wasn't expected to read what I was filing, but I did anyway. Even more after I talked with you. I think you're right. Something is going on there."

"Such as?"

"Well, I didn't find anything about a toxic dump, but once there was a letter from a window company owner and a second set of documents attached to it related to the bankruptcy of a Tucker subsidiary that the man's contract was actually with."

"What did the vendor letter say?"

"The owner was complaining that he wasn't getting the amount they agreed on for windows he had installed for one of Mr. Tucker's building projects. It said if he didn't get paid what was due he would take it to the state Attorney General."

"We heard something like that from another Tucker service provider who said pretty much the same thing. A lousy business practice, but not illegal."

"Yes, but then I overheard Mr. Tucker talking to one of those awful men he always has with him. It was a few months ago. He said he should 'take care of that guy'. I didn't think much of it at the time."

"By itself that could mean anything."

"I read the newspaper cover to cover every morning before I go to the office. A week or so after I overheard that I read a small story about a man who had left his house for work and never came home. The police said a thorough investigation showed there was no evidence of foul play. The man had been having financial problems. They assumed he abandoned his family."

"The same man?"

"Yes. That was when I suspected something was going on there. When you told me Mr. Tucker was a criminal, I put that incident together with what you said and I knew it was true."

She stopped talking when her hot chocolate arrived.

"So," Katt said, "If you put those things together it makes you wonder what 'take care of that guy' really meant."

"Exactly."

"Any chance of getting copies of those documents?"

Alice Simms reached inside her jacket and came out with a packet of folded papers."

"If they ever find out I gave you these I'm absolutely sure Mr. Tucker will have his men 'take care' of me."

"Okay, you have to stop right now. If you look as nervous to the people in your office as you look to me right now they are sure to wonder what's going on. I won't ask you for anything more. In fact, I absolutely don't want you to do anything else."

"Ms Li, I'm not a brave person. But I believe this is something I have to do."

Katt looked at the young woman and realized there was no way she could be discouraged from helping.

"If I can't talk you out of it, then I strongly suggest that you tell someone in your office that your boyfriend broke up with you and you haven't been able to sleep and you're a nervous wreck. That will get around. Maybe eliminate suspicion."

Alice looked down at her drink and said, "I've never had a boyfriend."

"They don't have to know that."

When Alice's sandwich arrived, it seemed like a good time for Katt to take off.

As she got up to leave Katt said, "Please. Don't take any chances. I don't want to be reading in the newspaper that you disappeared."

She dropped a twenty dollar bill on the table and left the young woman to deal with her fears.

"That girl has guts," Katt said when she got to the TV station.

Gary said, "Considering that Tucker's crew found everyone else we've been talking to, I think we should warn off Ms Simms."

"I did warn her, but she has made up her mind. We'll have to wait and see what she does."

Gary took out his cell phone and dialed Lou Wagner.

"It's Gary."

"I know it's Gary. You know how I know it's Gary? Because printed on my cell phone screen is the word 'Gary'."

"Can't sneak up on you, can I."

"I'd be surprised if you called me one day just to say hello and not to tell me you were risking your ass on some reckless adventure."

"Okay then. Hi Lou. Just called to say hello."

"Uh huh."

"And also to let you know we have a mole in our boy's office."

"Oh, Jesus mother Mary. Bad enough you're too dumb to stop putting your own neck on the chopping block, now you're getting other people involved."

"Katt tried to talk our spy out of any further involvement. Didn't do any good."

"You should be writing this stuff down. The soap operas are always looking for material."

"The mole already gave us some pretty damning evidence. I'll scan what we have. It includes some notes of mine about what it means. I'll email it to you and I'll let you know if we get anything else."

"Watch your back, buddy." He hung up.

"I'm really worried about Alice," Katt said. "I'm afraid they're going to get suspicious because of how jumpy she was. Her fear of getting killed could get her killed."

"It's out of our hands now," Jerry said. "All we can do is hope she doesn't get caught."

"Jerry, have you talked to Cheryl today?" Katt said.

"Yep. Janet is back on the job. Cheryl says they haven't seen anything suspicious so far this morning."

Gary was on his phone to Gus.

"It's Gary."

"I know it's Gary. You want to know how I know?"

"Because on your cell phone screen is the word 'Gary'."

"Aw, man."

"You having any fun with our project?"

"I am. I got some more."

"As they say in the fishing business, I await with baited breath."

Groans from Katt and Jerry.

"What have you got?"

"I got into Tucker's LAN. That's Local Area Network to you civilians."

"I know what a LAN is."

"Well I don't know everything you know and don't know."

"Duly noted. Anything that will put Mr. Tucker in jail? Better yet, the morgue?"

"Maybe. Something to piss him off, at least."

"Close enough. What have you got?"

"I found the offshore bank accounts. The idiot had a 'list' file among his documents that included account numbers and passwords.

Team Jerry did silent high fives.

"Theoretically you could get into those accounts."

"No 'theoretically' about it. With a couple of clicks I could be a very rich man."

"If you did that, would there be a way to trace it back to you?"

"It would take some doing, but possible. Better to trace it to you so I don't have some big ugly thug show up here looking for me."

"Since Tucker already knows we're onto him, what if we transferred one of those funds to Katt's account in the Caymans?"

"Very doable, mi amigo."

Gary turned to Katt, who nodded enthusiastically.

"How much money are we talking about?"

"Over two million in Liechtenstein; just under a half-million in a Cayman account."

"If it can't be tracked back to your computer, transfer the half mil to Katt."

Katt had jotted down her account information and Gary relayed it to Gus.

"The dinero is practically on its way. And may God have mercy on your souls."

"That's comforting. Let's make that two cases of Dos Equis, my friend."

"Maybe I'll just pay myself by transferring the two mil to my own account."

"I hope your lair can withstand a nuclear attack because that's what you could expect."

"Never mind then."

"Gracias. And then some. I'll keep you informed."

They broke the connection and Gary said, "Okay, we've engineered ourselves a little scrap of protection."

Katt's eyebrows went skyward. "How is stealing a half-million dollars protection for us?"

"Because if he were to kill us or cause harm to any of the people helping us he would never see that money again."

"Maybe we should have gone for the two million," Jerry said. "It might be worth a half-million dollars to him to be rid of us."

"You could be right," Katt said.

"It doesn't do any good to do something like this unless he knows we've done it," Gary said.

Katt went on the Internet to find a main number for Tucker's company, found it and gave it to Gary.

"Let's see if we can get through to his Highness," he said, using the TV station land line to make the call. He turned on the recorder.

A receptionist answered.

"Mr. Tucker please."

A few clicks and buzzes before being answered by a woman.

"Kathy Rankin."

"Ms Rankin, this is Gary Mansfield, TV Seven News. May I speak with Mr. Tucker please?"

There was a long pause. The kind Gary was accustomed to while the person he called was considering how to handle the call.

"I'm sorry, Mr. Mansfield, Mr. Tucker is not available right now."

"When would be a good time to call back. It's important that I speak directly to him."

"That's hard to say. As you might imagine, he is quite busy."

"Yes, so am I. Might I expect him to return my call?"

"Can you tell me what this is regarding?"

"It is a matter I believe he will find important."

"If I could just get some idea of what it is about."

"Look, Ms Rankin. It's obvious you have no intention of letting me talk to Mr. Tucker. So I will leave you with this. Tell him to check his Cayman account."

Without another word Gary hung up the phone.

"You didn't leave a number," Katt said.

"He will move heaven and earth to find me."

Gary looked at his watch. "I give it no more than 20 minutes."

In fact, it was just 18 minutes before the editing booth land line rang.

Gary turned the recorder on before he answered.

"Mansfield."

"What have you done, you sonofabitch?"

"What I have done is I have taken out an insurance policy against you and your little army ever again threatening my news team or anyone connected with us."

"How did you—"

"That is irrelevant. All you need to know is that you will never see that money again if your thugs come near any of us."

"I will have your job you arrogant bastard."

"Great. If I don't have to go to a job every day I'll have more time to investigate some of your more interesting activities. I won't need a salary because I recently acquired a small fortune to live off of."

"I don't know how you did it, but I want that money put right back where you found it."

"Maybe someday. Depends on whether you and your goons back off. I'll put it to you the way your guy did when he called us. 'You've been warned'."

Gary hung up the phone.

"We're in for it now," Jerry said.

"Maybe. Or maybe we'll get a break while Tucker tries to come up with a plan to get himself out from between a rock and a hard head."

Jerry got on his phone to Cheryl.

"Hi there."

"Hi yourself. Any activity?"

"Not a peep."

"You may get a little break. Meanwhile, let me talk to Janet. I'll explain it to her and she can tell you. That way I don't have to say it twice."

Jerry could hear Cheryl call out to Janet, who came to the phone.

"What's up handsome?"

Jerry gave Cheryl's protector a quick rundown on what they had done and what they might expect to happen as a result.

"One of two possibilities I can think of," Jerry said. "One is that you will get a little respite while Tucker is trying to figure it out. Second, all-out war."

"I don't know whether you are a genius or a freakin' idiot, but it is what it is, so we'll hope for the best and prepare for the worst."

"Right. Let me talk to Cheryl again."

Cheryl came back on the phone.

"That sounded ominous."

"We have done some things to unsettle Tucker. We figure he will respond in some way."

"Will you be okay?"

"I think so. It's you I worry about."

"I have the best protection. What have you got?"

"I have an armed, experienced ex-cop and a world class martial arts expert on my side. I would put them up against anyone. I didn't mention this before, but I am also armed."

"Still, please be careful."

"I will. And I'm really sorry about all this. Most guys, they meet a girl and they have dinner, maybe go to a movie, talk and laugh. I had to be different. I will make this up to you."

"As Janet said, 'it is what it is'. I think we're worth it."

"I'll talk to you later. Bye."

<u>EIGHTEEN</u>

Maybe we should take out Tucker's army before they have a chance to harm her," Gary said.

"I have never wanted to destroy someone more in my life," Katt said.

"We couldn't walk right up to them and shoot them, but self-defense would work."

"Okay, Anything to get rid of them."

"How about we draw them out. We put them in a position where we have no choice but to fight back?"

"Works for me."

Gary called Lester Manning.

"How'd you like to take part in a showdown?"

"Beats sittin' around waiting for the other shoe to drop."

Gary thought Manning was also thinking, but not saying, "beats sitting around waiting to die."

Gary did not hesitate for a second to get Manning involved. If anyone could handle what Gary had in mind, it would be an ex Navy Seal who was convinced he was going to die anyway. Nothing on earth is more dangerous than a man with nothing to lose.

"I'll make them think I'm going to the dump site to take samples."

"Where and when?"

"Now. Gun up."

"We should get there before them."

"We're on our way to your place."

"You'll have to sit this one out," Jerry.

"I sit everything out, Gary. But I know what you mean."

"I'm not crazy about your going along, Katt."

"Don't even think about going without me."

"Twenty minutes later, Katt and Gary were at Manning's house. He was standing at the curb waiting for them.

The van had barely stopped when he jumped into a rear seat and they were on their way.

When they arrived at the road that ran alongside the Sierra Estates property Gary parked his van out of sight and they walked to the dump site.

He called Tucker and had to endure the usual Kathy Rankin attitude. But he was finally put through to Tucker.

"Now what?"

"Let's see how you explain all the poisons you put in the ground. I'm gonna go out there and take samples and get them to the right people. Talk your way out of that, hotshot."

He hung up.

They settled down on the forest floor with a good view of the clearing.

"Now we wait," Gary said.

Gary had his tiny buttonhole camera with him. A record of any confrontation might be helpful if they had to prove self-defense.

Not more than twenty minutes after Gary made the call they heard the crunching of leaves in the direction of the road. Gary, Katt, and Lester lay flat against the forest floor.

The men who had been identified as Joseph Carnahan and Melvin Gingrich emerged with guns drawn. Seeing no one, they started walking beyond the clearing to set up an ambush.

Gary called out, "Looking for us, fellas?"

Both men spun toward the voice. Gingrich raised his gun, but never got a chance to fire it, because he was hit in the chest by two 9 millimeter rounds from Lester's Glock and his head took one from Gary's Makarov.

One down, one to go.

Carnahan fired blindly in their direction, missing by a comfortable margin. As he backed out of the clearing, Lester's shot struck him in the chest. Gary's round hit a shoulder. It didn't stop him from getting away.

Katt jumped to her feet to pursue.

"No, Katt," Gary shouted. "It would have been self-defense when he was shooting at us. If you kill him now it would be murder."

"He'll still be coming after us," she said.

"We reduced Tucker's army by half."

"Don't count on it," Lester said. "There are plenty more renegade ex special forces types willing to do dirty work. Some of them go the hired gun route when they separate from the military."

Gary was on the phone.

"Lou, we just got into a gunfight with Tucker's thugs. One's dead, one got away."

"You okay?"

"Yeah. And I have video to prove self-defense."

"Where are you?"

"At the Tucker development site."

There was a long pause at Wagner's end.

"Let me understand this. You trespassed on Tucker property and Tucker's security men found you there?"

"Uh."

"I believe right in here somewhere is where you say—"

"Oh, shit!"

"The video evidence you have might prove Tucker's case against you better than yours against him."

"Now what do I do?"

"About what?"

"About killing a guy on private property."

"I have no idea what you're talking about, Gary. I think we have a bad connection."

"Talk to you later, Lou."

Each of them had taken lives before; Manning in war, Gary as a cop and in his battle against the Russian mob. Katt had killed one of the Russians who kidnapped her. While it always affected a person when they took a life, even when that person deserved to die, there was some comfort in knowing that an evil man had been taken out of circulation.

They left the corpse where he fell and walked cautiously back to Gary's van, keeping a wary eye on possible hiding places for Carnahan in case he decided to ambush them on their way out. Off somewhere licking his wounds, they assumed.

"This never happened, Lester," Gary said.

"Then why do I feel so good?"

They took Lester home and went back to the station where they filled Jerry in on what happened in the woods.

<u>NINETEEN</u>

They had just arrived at the station and barely settled in when Stan Hawkins burst into the editing booth.

"You three, this way," he said, gesturing for them to follow him.

Instead of heading for the conference room for a meeting of the field reporting teams, Hawkins led them in a different direction.

Reporter Dennis Murphy looked their way and shrugged, indicating he didn't know what was going on.

"Now what," Katt whispered.

"Nothing good," Gary said.

"Hawkins is smiling," Jerry said. "That's never a good thing."

When they were standing in front of the general manager's office, Hawkins motioned for them to go in.

"Oh, shit," Katt said.

As they passed by Hawkins he whispered, "You're toast, Mansfield."

General Manager Cyrus Weaver was a stern man in the best of times. On this occasion he had multiplied that persona by hundreds. Standing behind his oversized desk with his arms folded, red-faced, looking very much like he might explode,

It was not hard to figure out why they were there.

"I got a call from a Mr. Alexander Tucker. Do you by any chance know who Alexander Tucker is?"

Nods.

"Mr. Alexander "Alex" Tucker is one of Carsonville's leading citizens. He is noted for his philanthropy and his contributions to the city's economy by providing jobs and by generating tax revenues. Does that name ring a bell?"

More nods.

I got a call from Mr. Tucker. And do you know what Mr. Leading Citizen said to me?"

Weaver waited a moment for dramatic effect, looking from face to face.

"He said one of my field reporting teams was slandering his good name by accusing him of unethical, perhaps illegal, business practices."

Stan Hawkins was nearly suffocating himself trying not to smirk.

"Is that true?"

Gary was the first to speak.

"Absolutely, one-hundred-percent. But we did not accuse him publically, just to him personally."

Weaver clenched his fists and leaned on his desk.

"Are you even slightly aware of the benefits Mr. Tucker brings to the Carsonville economy? How in God's name could you possibly think you could get away with something like that?"

"Mr. Weaver—" Gary said.

"Quiet! I'll call on you when I want you to speak," the head man said.

"Sorry, I thought that was a question."

"Yes. All right, speak."

"Alex Tucker is a criminal and quite possibly a murderer. What's more, we are well on our way to proving it."

"That is absurd. The man has done nothing but good for this community over the past fifteen years."

"On the surface, that appears to be true. But dig a little deeper and you will find that he is guilty of some of the worst business practices imaginable, including cheating his subcontractors out of money due their services, dumping deadly chemicals into the acreage where he is planning to build homes, Oh, and murder."

"Impossible!"

"Mr. Weaver," Jerry said. "Alex Tucker has men working for him who do his dirty work. Right at this moment a good friend of ours is being threatened in order to make us stop our investigation. As we speak, we have an armed guard watching over her because of threats that have been made. We stopped them from murdering a man who has provided us with information about that dump site. Gary's apartment was firebombed Wednesday night."

"What evidence do you have that it was them?"

"We confronted those thugs who work for him within fifty feet of the informant's home. The police have a record of it and I have a picture of the two of them.

Gary pulled out his cell phone and brought up the photo to show Weaver.

We have a growing body of solid evidence," Katt said. "Documents, testimony, video, plus a lot of things we are absolutely sure of, but can't yet prove."

"Well there you have it. You can't prove it, yet you are willing to destroy a man's good name, which you will stop immediately or you can start looking for jobs somewhere else."

Gary couldn't stand it any longer. He leaned on his fists on Weaver's desk to match the manager's stance and looked the man straight in his eyes."

"If you force us to stop our investigation, you will, in effect, be an accomplice to a long list of crimes. Is that what you want, Mr. Weaver?"

Weaver's face went slack.

"How is that? I have done nothing."

"Exactly," Katt said. "You will have done nothing to stop a criminal from continuing his crimes after you became aware of the facts."

"But you admitted that most of what you have is suspicions."

Jerry said, "We don't have all of the facts, but we do have quite a few. Plus there is enough more to convince us this is worth digging into. Our suspicions are based on hard-earned experience with the man: threats by Tucker and his hirelings and eye-witness accounts of their attacks on our friends."

"Finding stories that affect Carsonville residents is what we are supposed to be doing," Katt said.

Weaver turned to Hawkins.

"Stan, were you aware that these three were investigating Tucker?"

Hawkins had lost his smile.

"I warned them to stop, but they wouldn't."

"And this is the first time I've heard anything about this?"

"Well, yes. I didn't want to trouble you with—"

"How long have you known about this?"

"Uh. A couple of weeks."

"And you didn't think it was important enough to bring it to me?"

Hawkins had completely lost the smirk he had been enjoying.

"They threatened me, Mr. Weaver. They threatened to spread it around that I was keeping them from investigating. Mansfield said I would never get a job in news again if it got around that I wouldn't let them investigate."

"So, for personal reasons you failed to bring a major issue to my attention for a decision that was not yours to make?"

"Well, I—"

"Go back to your desk, Stan. We'll talk more about this later."

Hawkins turned and started toward his desk. He hesitated for a moment and half turned around.

"Now, Stan," Weaver said.

As the news director passed by, Gary whispered, "You're toast, Hawkins,"

Katt was trying very hard not to adopt the smirk Hawkins had lost. She was failing miserably.

"Sit down." Weaver said. "Tell me more about these suspicions."

Team Jerry spent the next hour relating to the head man everything they could without compromising the investigation: the firebombing, the interview with their whistleblower, the attack on Cheryl resulting in the need for security guards at her home, their nighttime trip to the hazardous waste site, and the results of the lab tests on what they found at the proposed Sierra Estates tract.

What they did not tell Weaver was that they'd had a source inside the Tucker organization and that they had killed one of Tucker's thugs and wounded another.

Also absent from their briefing was the fact that they had hijacked a half-million dollars from Tucker's Cayman Islands account.

Weaver paced behind his desk, deep in thought.

"All right," he said. "I want you to continue what you've been doing. But, before we can absolutely prove any of it, we must keep it quiet. For one thing, Tucker is a very litigious individual. I don't want to spend the rest of my life in courtrooms. For another, we don't want to get a reputation for what might appear to be tabloid journalism."

"Is Hawkins to be any part of this?" Gary said.

"No. He will be instructed to take you off the regular assignment rotation. I would appreciate it if you could occasionally turn in a feature, just to keep your image alive for the audience. However, you may come and go as you see fit and you will report directly to me, understood?"

"Understood," Gary said. "But you must understand that whatever we report to you will have to be after the fact. We will not be asking for permission every time we have to take a certain course of action. That would slow us down too much.

"I can live with that. Within reason."

The three filed out of the office and returned to the editing booth. On the way they saw Hawkins walking toward Cyrus Weaver's office and the door close.

With the door to the soundproof booth shut behind them, Katt said, "I think Alex needs another lesson in the cost of threatening us."

"My thought exactly," Jerry said.

"I'll call Gus," Gary said.

Three people, one brain. The benefit of working so closely for so long.

One ring and Gus was on the line.

"Did you miss me?"

"Terribly, my friend. How quickly could you move Alex's two million dollar Liechtenstein account to Katt's account—assuming it's still there?"

Gary could hear clicking of a keyboard. In less than a minute, Gus was back.

"It was still there, but it isn't any more. Was that fast enough?"

"You are one amazing Mexican, Deserving of yet another case of Dos Equis."

"Ieeeee. I am rich!"

High fives all around.

"I was afraid Alex might have moved his Liechtenstein account," Gary said. "We caught it before he did."

"I think we can expect another phone call soon," Jerry said.

"Why wait? Let's call him and record it."

Gary was on the phone again, the call on the speaker.

Jerry reached over and flipped on a recorder.

"Kathy Rankin, please."

"One moment please."

Three rings.

"Kathy Rankin."

"Alex Tucker, please. Gary Mansfield calling."

"You!"

"Yes, me. Put the call through and do it fast."

Heavy breathing on the other end of the line, but in the end she transferred the call.

"This is Alex."

"Some people have to learn the hard way. I told you not to mess with me and mine, but you had to call the TV station manager to try to make life difficult for us."

"It was my pleasure, you bastard."

"Well, let me demonstrate for you the high cost of being a dick."

"Jesus Christ, what have you done now?"

"Check your Liechtenstein account."

"You didn't! Oh, dear God. You didn't."

"As a matter of actual fact, I did. My war chest is growing, Alex. Fling something at us, we will fling back. Money is no object. I will be using two-and-a-half million dollars of your money as ammunition."

"I will bury you. They will never find your body."

"You mean like those people you screwed out of money and when they objected you had them killed? How many of those were there? You are not planning to let us live anyway. I don't see where this changes anything. Except you will be millions of dollars poorer because if we are dead we can't return it."

"The difference now is that the three of you will die slowly and very painfully. Make that four. We'll take the girlfriend first."

"The only way you will ever see that money again is if we four remain in good health."

Gary hung up the phone and put a copy of the conversation into the Tucker file.

"He's never getting that money back anyway," Katt said. "And he knows it. So there is nothing much to keep him from going after us now."

"Jerry, we have to get Cheryl moved to a safe place."

"What about her business?"

"We'll transfer all of her phone lines to a place that Tucker couldn't get to with a fleet of tanks."

"That could work. If she's willing."

"You will have to convince her."

<u>TWENTY</u>

I don't know why we bother to come to the station," Katt said when they arrived. "Weaver told us we can come and go as we please. We could work from home and avoid all the office BS."

"Might miss some phone calls," Gary said. "There is a flow of information here that we can benefit from."

Jerry said, "We should talk to the wife of that window guy who went missing."

"Katt," Gary said, "did your mole give you any idea of when he disappeared?"

"No, but we could check the newspaper archives for the article she mentioned."

Jerry went to the computer. "I'll see if Mister Google can find anything about Carsonville missing persons."

Within minutes Jerry had a list of the missing. "California alone had about two-thousand people disappear without a trace last year," Jerry said

Katt, who was once a missing person herself when she ran away from foster care in her teens, said, "People disappear for a lot of reasons: Abused kids and spouses, parents who kidnap their own children after they lose custody, people drowning in debt. All kinds of reasons. Some people drop out because they hate their life. Some because someone is out to do them harm. And I'm sure there are those who are pushing up cactus out in the desert."

"Don't forget UFO abductions," Gary said."

Katt rolled her eyes.

"Found it," Jerry said. "It says, 'Vincent Noonan, 48, owner of Noonan Windows, went to his place of business the morning of August 12th, but did not return home that evening. He was still unaccounted for the following day. His wife, Jean Noonan, reported her husband missing. Carsonville police Chief Lester Magee says Mr. Noonan had suffered crippling businesses losses. Chief Magee released a statement saying: 'absent evidence of foul play, our investigators have concluded that Mr. Noonan left the area to avoid his creditors'. Noonan's wife was quoted as saying,

'Vincent would never walk out on his debts or on me. He is an honorable man and we have a wonderful relationship'. Detectives assigned to the case have ended their investigation."

"Any bets on whether Mr. Noonan is still alive?" Gary said.

"Considering our own experience with Tucker's stooges," Katt said, "I'd say odds are running against it."

"I found a phone number for a V.A. Noonan." Jerry said. No address,"

Katt made the call. A woman answered.

"Mrs. Noonan?"

"Yes."

"Was it your husband who disappeared several months ago?"

"Yes," she said excitedly. *"Do you have some information?"*

"Nothing specific, ma'am. This is Katt Li from TV News Seven. I wondered if we might come by your home and talk with you?"

"I suppose that would be all right. When would you be coming?"

"We can be there in less than an hour."

Mrs. Noonan gave Katt the address.

Gary gathered up his camera gear and Team Jerry headed out.

Stan Hawkins glowered at them as they passed him in the newsroom. It looked as though the manager's little talk with the news director did some good.

They took Gary's van, even though loading Jerry and his wheelchair was more difficult to handle than with the satellite truck's chair lift.

"We gotta get a lift on this van," Katt said.

Jerry smiled. "You could pay for it with Alex Tucker's money."

It was a short trip and they were at the Noonan residence barely 20 minutes after Katt spoke with the woman.

Jean Noonan lived in an upper middle class neighborhood in east Carsonville. The Noonan residence was a large brick affair set back from the street. The lawn needed mowed. The house was typical of those built in the 1930s. The street was lined with similar homes, but neater lawns.

"A TV station truck in front of a house would have attracted a lot of attention," Katt said. "She doesn't need that."

An attractive woman in her late forties answered the door.

After introductions the woman guided them inside and they were offered a seat in the living room of the tidy home.

"Thank you for seeing us, Mrs. Noonan," Katt said.

"Do you have any new information at all," she said.

"No," Katt said, "but we would like to help locate your husband. I guess the question I have is, what do you think happened to him?"

Mrs. Noonan looked like a woman who had not smiled in some time. Her face had lines that might be expected in a much older person. Recently acquired, Katt assumed.

"I believe the only reason Vincent would not have returned home—" She struggled to hold back a sob. "—is because he is dead."

"What makes you think that?"

"Vincent and I are very close. He simply would not leave me like that."

Jerry said, "Have you given any thought to exactly how he might have died? If he died."

Jean Noonan got very quiet. She seemed to be growing angry.

"Please understand, I have no proof. But I think Alex Tucker's people had something to do with it."

Katt, Gary, and Jerry exchanged glances.

"Based on what, Mrs. Noonan?"

"Please don't repeat this to anyone. I could be sued and I have very little money. I've been living on savings since the business shut down. There's not much left. I can't even afford the basics, like lawn care. The house had been nearly paid off, but we took a second mortgage for a new roof and some upgrades. It has been hard to make the payments. I'm about to lose my home."

"Why do you believe Tucker was involved?"

"He refused to pay the full 28-thousand dollars he owed for a job my husband did in one of the Tucker projects. We ended up getting nothing. Vincent threatened to take his complaint to state authorities. It was just a week later that my husband vanished."

"Mrs. Noonan," Gary said, "you have just said what the three of us have been thinking."

"You do know something, don't you?"

"We know some things," Katt said, "and we suspect some things we can't prove yet."

"Please tell me. I die a little every day not knowing."

Katt considered whether it was worse that the woman was in more pain from not knowing than she would be to hear what they believe to be the truth. She decided that knowing was the better choice.

As gently as she could, Katt said, "I'm sorry to say that we also believe your husband is dead."

The only sound in that moment was the ticking of the grandfather clock in a corner of the living room.

The woman nodded slowly. Tears flowed down her cheeks.

Jerry said, "Tucker has a history of short-changing vendors and subcontractors. Two men who work for him have threatened us and friends of ours. They don't want us to investigate Tucker for immoral business practices."

Katt said, "It's not too big a leap to imagine that, if they are willing to threaten to kill us for investigating them locally where they have officials in their pocket, then the prospect of an investigation by state authorities which they have no control over might drive them to murder."

"Mrs. Noonan," Gary said. "It is very important that you not share what we have told you with anyone just yet. It could hamper our investigation and we really want to stop this monster."

"Can't I even tell my sister? She lives in Minnesota."

"Best not to. I know it's hard to keep it inside of you. Not only could it upset the investigation, it could put you—and us—in mortal danger. Secrets have a funny way of getting around to the wrong people. Just to be safe, please don't tell anyone, no matter how great the temptation, no matter how much you think it wouldn't matter."

"There is no one here I would tell."

Gary signaled to his teammates that it was time to go. They got up and walked to the door.

"Thank you for taking the time to talk with us," Katt said. "We will let you know if we learn anything. In the meantime, as Gary said, it is absolutely vital that you not say anything to anyone."

Back in the van, Jerry said, "do you think she'll tell anyone?"

"Of course," Katt said. "She's bursting to tell someone there has been progress, even though there really has not been. She'll call her sister in Minnesota who will call someone else who will call someone in Carsonville, who will spread it faster than a virus."

"We have to get busy," Jerry said.

"I talked to Cheryl," Jerry said. "She still says she doesn't want to move."

Gary got on his cell phone.

"Pat. Could you provide two guards again on a regular basis for our girl round the clock?"

"A bit of a stretch, but we can do it. ?"

"The threat has increased a thousand-fold."

"Christ, Gary. Why don't you just move the girl somewhere that would be impossible to penetrate?"

"She doesn't want to leave her house and we understand her reasons."

"Okay. I'll get a man over there right now."

"Good. By the way, Cheryl and Janet have become practically blood sisters. Janet would fend off an all-out attack by herself."

"She'd have done that even if they weren't friends. Janet has quite a resume. She was one of the first of the female Army Green Berets. She is both the friendliest person—and a terrifying fighting machine. It's like she has an OFF/ON switch. You wouldn't want to be on her bad side when the switch is ON."

"Good to know. Keep our girl safe."

"We will do our best."

"Even Tucker's thugs can't get past Pat's people," Gary said.

What else can we do to irritate Tucker?" Jerry said.

Katt had an idea. "Why don't we tinker with the Tucker company computers?"

"I wonder who we could get to do that." Jerry said.

Gary was already making the call.

"Hola, Gary."

"Gus, you wouldn't happen to have a nasty virus you might infect Mr. Tucker's LAN with would you?"

"Funny you should ask. I have a modified version of one the North Koreans tried to get into American government systems. It didn't work, of course. Our geeks were smarter than their geeks and we out-nerded them. I made some improvements. I would be happy to share it with Mr. Tucker."

"Can they remove it?"

"With my refinements they won't even be able to find it. Only I will be able to reverse it"

"What will it do to their system?"

"When they type a letter, number, or character the virus will input a different letter, number, or character. The bug will lock up all files so they can't be deleted, changed, or even accessed. But we can."

"Perfect, because some day we are going to want to see those files."

Gary promised another case of Mexican beer.

"At this rate, Dos Equis is gonna have to go to extra shifts to keep up with the load."

"You're worth every last bubble, my friend. Later."

Jerry started toward the newsroom.

"I want to be with Cheryl," Jerry said.

"She has plenty of protection, Jer."

"Besides," Katt said, "we need your input in planning."

"With cell phones it would be like I'm with you. I really want to be there."

"I understand," Gary said.

"Me too," Katt said. "We'll miss having you here, but we get it."

Jerry spun his chair around and was gone.

"Maybe we should all be there," Katt said.

"Gotta keep our eyes on the prize."

The sun had just slipped beyond the western horizon when Jerry arrived at Cheryl's home. She greeted him enthusiastically at the door. Her two guardians did not immediately show themselves.

"I'm so glad you're here," she said. "You met Janet. That's Frank.

"We're up to strength now," Janet said. "Welcome to the stronghold. Pull up a shotgun and stay awhile."

"Got my own weapon," Jerry said, bringing out his Colt Mustang.

Janet made a face like she had eaten something sour.

"Ha! That little squirter would just piss 'em off," Janet said. "You want something like this."

She reached into a military type bag and pulled out a Colt .45 Model 1911 semi automatic. She handed it to him butt first.

"Works the same as your peashooter, just sends a louder message."

"A very nice gift, Janet. Thank you."

"It's a loaner, Ace," she said, shaking a fist at him. "I'll want it back when this business is taken care of."

"Darn, and I had already become attached to it."

Cheryl said, "with luck you won't need any of it."

Janet shook her head. "I don't believe in luck, baby doll."

"Well, I'm lucky to have you here," Cheryl said.

"Are you sure you aren't too nice for this job, Janet?" Jerry said with a huge smile.

Frank laughed out loud, but he stopped when Janet turned a hot glare on him..

"I mean, if Tucker has hired new thugs and they show up, we don't want to greet them with a Welcome Wagon gift basket," Jerry said.

"How's this for a gift basket, wise-ass?" she said, patting the shotgun slung over a massive shoulder.

The words were no sooner out of her mouth than a heavy object came out of the darkness, crashing through the living room's picture window and thudding on the floor.

As though Janet's switch had suddenly flipped to ON, she dove for the object, threw it back through the shattered pane with the deftness of a second baseman scooping a ball to first for the out just an instant before the object erupted, sending shards of steel in every direction.

At the same instant, Frank had put himself between the grenade and Cheryl, grabbed the back of her wheelchair, and pushed her at top speed away from the living room before the grenade went off. Jerry was close behind.

Janet was out the door, looking for the bomber.

With several walls between them and the outdoors, Jerry was on the phone to Gary.

"How you doing?"

"Fine, except for the grenade that was just thrown through the front window."

"Christ! You and Cheryl okay?"

"We're fine, thanks to Janet and Frank's quick action. She jumped on the grenade and threw it back before it went off. It was amazing."

"I don't know how much Pat is paying her, but it's not enough,"

"Apparently Tucker's army is back up to strength. We've got to take those guys out. "

"Gus's virus will hit in the morning. I'll let Tucker know the price went up again. Are those sirens I hear?"

"Yep. I guess a neighbor called the cops to report the blast. How am I going to explain it?"

"Tell them someone threw a grenade through the window. You don't have to give them a lot of details. I'll call Lou and get him to take care of it."

"Okay," he said as Janet came back inside. "I'll hide the bodyguards."

Jerry went out to meet the police. Neighbors were standing in their yards to see what the ruckus was all about.

One man spotted Jerry. "Hey, you're that TV guy. What happened?" he said.

"A big firecracker, I think," Jerry said.

"I never heard a cherry bomb that loud before."

"Kids today, huh?" Jerry said.

"Why would they do that to Cheryl?" he said. "There isn't a nicer person anywhere."

The cruiser screeched to a stop and two officers jumped out and approached the house.

Jerry went to meet them, out of earshot of the neighbor.

"What happened?"

"Somebody threw a grenade through the window," Jerry said.

"Any idea who did it?"

"We have our suspicions,"

Jerry's phone rang.

Lou Wagner's name came on the screen..

"I have to take this."

"Jerry, it's Lou. Police there?"

"Yes," Jerry said, reading the name tag on the cop's shirt, "It's Officer Brunner."

"Lemme talk to him."

Jerry handed the phone to the cop and said, "It's Detective Lou Wagner."

"Yeah, Lou. Uh huh, . . . uh huh."

Brunner nodded without saying anything for awhile.

"Detective, this wouldn't happen to be connected to that stop I made a couple of nights ago? The two thugs we confronted with that ex-cop?"

Brunner again went quiet for a moment, then handed the phone back to Jerry.

"Brunner is one of the guys I put on watch at your girlfriend's place and the whistleblower's. He'll write this up as a prank."

"Thanks, Lou."

"Everybody okay? No injuries?"

"None, thanks to Supergirl. If I hadn't seen what Janet did with my own eyes I would have believed it."

"I asked Brunner and his partner to pay extra special attention to this place until further notice."

"We appreciate it. Thanks, Lou."

The cop stuck his thumbs in his gun belt and looked very serious.

"Somebody really has it in for you guys," Brunner said.

"Those men you ran into the other night with Katt and Gary don't like that we're doing an investigation of their crooked business practices."

"Detective Wagner says you have some security."

"The best. They saved our girl's life tonight."

Jerry very carefully did not mention the name Tucker. He thanked the officers for coming and watched them drive away. On the way back inside he saw what the grenade had done to the front of the house. The picture window was smashed and the siding and door were pocked with tiny holes. He made a mental note to himself to have a repair crew fix it.

"I'm staying here with you," he said.

Cheryl squeezed his hand and smiled.

Janet's ON switch had not quite turned off yet. She still had fire in her eyes.

"You're due to go off duty, Janet," Jerry said.

"I'm no leaving here until I know our girl is safe."

"Tucker must have hired some new thugs because one of the originals is dead and the other is shot up and we don't know where he is or if he's still alive."

All lights except one small lamp with a low wattage bulb were off in the living room and Frank was pacing in the semi-darkness. The only illumination outside was from a streetlight halfway down the block.

"We gotta get some cameras outside," Frank said. "Front and back."

"I have a better idea," Janet said. "We could just hunt those guys down."

"It's been suggested," Jerry said. "The problem is, there are plenty of replacements available."

TWENTY-ONE

The TV station manager buzzed Team Jerry's booth.
"Could you come to my office?"
"On our way" Gary said and hung up.
"Now what?" Katt said.
"It's never good when you get called to the office," Gary said. "I learned that in elementary school."
Unlike their previous call on the carpet, Cyrus Weaver sat behind his desk looking very tired.
"I got a call from the Mayor. He says he and the police chief want to know why we are investigating Alex Tucker."
"Did you tell him?" Gary said.
"Not in great detail. I just said there was reason to believe Tucker was engaged in some illegal activity."
Katt said, "I'll bet he told you to cease and desist."
"That is exactly what he said, though not in those words. I don't use the words he used."
"And you said . . .?"
"I asked him what his reaction would be if I told him I wanted the city police to stop one of their investigations. While he was muttering something about a TV station not being authorized to conduct criminal investigations I reminded him of the Constitutional guarantee of a free press."
"Let me guess," Gary said. "He was not impressed or dissuaded."
"That was precisely his position."
"Don't you think it's kind of strange that a mayor would discourage an investigation into shady dealings of a business in his city?"
The question was rhetorical, but Gary wanted to see Weaver's reaction to it.
"Not at all," the manager said. "His is an elective office. Tucker is generous with his political contributions and His Honor would not want that money source to dry up."
"Justice be damned," Katt said.

"I think the mayor should be included in what you're looking into."

"And the chief," Katt said. "The mayor is elected, but the chief keeps that job at the will of the mayor."

"Or," Gary said, "the chief is outright on the take."

"It begs closer examination," Weaver said.

"If this was a popularity contest, I think we'd lose," Katt said.

"I've stopped thinking about what people think of us in favor of doing our civic duty," Weaver said. "I just hope this can be wrapped up soon."

"We'll do our best to end this quickly," Gary said. "Sorry to say, another call could be coming from Tucker today."

"Dear God. What now?"

"To combat his attack on us, we have put a virus in his corporate computer network to freeze his files and to make it impossible to input, delete, or retrieve any data."

"How in the world did—never mind. I don't want to know."

Weaver gave them a weak wave as they left his office.

"Who'da thought it," Katt said. "The manager is an actual human."

"He's taking a big risk with the bean counters who own this station. His job depends on profits. Lawsuits could cost a mint."

"I think we should call young Mr. Tucker, Katt said.

Gary got on the editing booth phone.

When Tucker came on the line the rage oozed through the phone line.

"You bastards. You did this."

"Call it repayment for your thugs' attack last night. Just another example of the high cost of screwing with us. It's like Isaac Newton said: 'Every action has an equal and opposite reaction'. You mess with us, we mess with you."

Only heavy breathing could be heard at Tucker's end.

"We have lots more tricks in our bag, Tucker. Call them off or suffer the consequences."

More heavy breathing."

Tucker hung up without a word.

"So," Katt said, "he's going to stop the attacks and be a sweetie."

"No, I think he's going to go kamikaze. He knows he's lost the money and all he has left is revenge."

"We have to find those guys."

"We have a couple of other things to do first," Gary said.

"Okay . . ."

"Can you get some of Alex's money out of your off-shore account?"

"Nothing to it. What do you have in mind?"

"To make Jean Noonan's life easier."

Katt called Mrs. Noonan and explained that she could receive the money Tucker bilked them out of.

"We know you're in a financial crunch because of all of this," Gary said. "So we have prepared a little relief for you."

"I would need the numbers from your checking account," Katt said. "That way I can make the transfer."

"Wait just a minute and I'll get the company checkbook."

Katt called Gus with the numbers and had him transfer 38-thousand dollars to the Noonan account from the Tucker money.

"That was ten-thousand dollars more than Tucker owed," Katt said. "But she had nearly exhausted her savings because of being cheated out of their money."

That done, Katt called Mrs. Noonan again to explain what she had done. She asked her to check her account when the bank logged the deposit.

"My Lord, where did the money come from? Is this real?"

"It came from Alex Tucker in a roundabout way that he would not approve of," Gary said. "It should take some of the financial pressure off you for living expenses and mortgage payments for awhile. You will have to declare that as business income, but the business losses should more than offset it."

Katt could hear the woman crying softly.

"It is important that you don't mention this to anyone," Katt said. "If it got out that it's Tucker's money and he got wind of it, your life could be in danger. Just like if you told anyone about you giving us information in our investigation."

"You didn't tell anyone, did you?" Gary said.

Jean Noonan didn't say anything right away.

"Ohmygod," Katt said. "You told someone."

"Only my sister, but she's all the way to Minnesota. That's far from here."

"You would be surprised how small this country is when it comes to secrets spreading," Gary said. "Human nature makes people blab everything they know. If they have been told it's a secret, it spreads even faster."

"You can bet that if Alex Tucker has not already heard that you have talked to us, then he soon will," Jerry said.

"You are in danger, Mrs. Noonan," Katt said. "All you had to do was to keep this to yourself. Now I believe you should leave town as soon as possible. Maybe go stay with your sister."

"I don't see why . . ."

"We've said all we are going to say about it," Gary said. "What you do now is up to you. We won't be contacting you again. I wish you luck because you are going to need it."

Katt gave the woman her cell phone number.

"Call me when you are in a safe place. If we don't hear from you, we will assume the worst."

Katt hung up the phone.

"I think we may just have been talking to a dead woman," Katt said.

"She won't feel threatened until those guys have guns pointed at her."

Jerry called from Cheryl's.

"Cheryl has reconsidered a move. When I told her the security guards were also at risk, she caved."

Gary and Katt jumped into action and arranged for a more secure, more defensible place and to have all the phone lines transferred. In mere hours, calling in many favors to get it done, Cheryl was transferred to what amounted to a fortress.

Not that the place was without charm. It was a perfectly livable two bedroom ground floor apartment on a cul de sac. The advantages were that it was a hardened shelter, and that Tucker did not know where it was located.

"Walls of poured concrete and all the comforts of home," Katt said.

"Even if Tucker's guys knew where she was," Gary said, "nothing can penetrate these walls."

"Now that I'm sure she's safe I'll be rejoining you," Jerry said.

"All for one, one for all," Katt shouted.

Gary called Pat Anderson.

"We can cut the guards back to one, Pat," Gary said.

"Good. A second body for three shifts was putting a strain on our force."

"Just be sure to leave Janet and Frank on the team."

"I doubt Janet would leave if I ordered her to."

TWENTY-TWO

I forgot to tell you," Gary said. "I bought a bigger gun."

"Where is it"\?" Katt said.

"I'll pick it up tomorrow. There's a ten-day waiting period for guns. That way you can't get pissed at your boss, buy a gun and go shoot him. You have to stay pissed for ten days and then go shoot him."

"What did you get," Jerry said.

"It's a 1991 Colt .45. Same caliber as the one Janet loaned you, but a later model."

"What are you gonna do with the Makarov?"

"I'll give it to Lou and confess I stole it from a Russian mobster. I never felt right about it anyway."

"You guys and your guns," Katt said. "You will never know the joy of pounding the crap out of a bad guy, the sheer delight of slamming them up against a wall, the feel of snapping bones, the orgasmic pleasure of administering violent skull fracturing justice on the spot."

Gary and Jerry looked at Katt in absolute horror.

"What?" Katt said.

TWENTY-THREE

I've been looking at the map of Tucker's proposed development," Gary said.

The newspaper had published a double-page color spread of Sierra Estates the day after Alex Tucker announced it.

"If my calculations are right, the waste dump would remain a wooded patch with a nature trail running through it."

"That would cover over the toxics, but it would still leak into the groundwater," Jerry said.

"I had a thought," Katt said.

"Oh no!" Gary said.

"Brace yourself, Gary," Jerry said, holding on to the computer desk.

"Shut up. You remember I said I wondered what else might be buried out there."

"Lester also suggested there might be bodies buried in those woods. I wonder what Lou and Hank would think of it.

Gary called Lou Wagner and put the call on the speaker.

"Lou, I'd like to run an idea by you."

"Does it have to do with your playing cop?"

"Yes, it does. Except it's Katt's idea."

"Oh, well, in that case, let me hear it."

"Thank you for your support. She thinks there might be something else buried in that site on the Tucker property."

"Something like . . ."

"Like, maybe, dead bodies."

"What evidence do you have?"

"Absolutely none."

"The D.A. wouldn't touch it and no judge would issue a warrant based on a hunch."

"What about the audio tapes?"

"Some question about whether they were legally obtained."

"Okay," Gary said. "But when you consider that we know that some people connected to Tucker have disappeared, it's worth keeping this in our back pocket for when we can nail the S.O.B."

"Yeah, there's a good chance Katt's right about dead bodies. She's a lot smarter than you. Did you know that?"

"I do know that and I'm okay with it. Especially since she's standing right behind me."

"Bye Katt."

"Bye, Lou," Katt yelled.

"No word from our mole," Gary said.

"No, and I'm worried." Katt said. "I'll go to the restaurant. She's there every day."

Katt braved the restaurant's fumes, took up her regular spot and waited.

But Alice Simms had not showed up at her usual time, nor had she appeared an hour-and-a-half later. Katt waited until 1:30 before she gave up.

She called Gary.

"No show. Now I'm really worried."

"Try again tomorrow. Could be a good reason she didn't come today."

"I got her into this. I'll never forgive myself if something has happened to her."

"Hey, you tried to talk her out of it."

Katt returned to the station.

The editing booth land line rang. Gary had made it a practice to record all incoming calls. He switched on the digital recorder.

"Mansfield."

"Now you will learn the cost of screwing with me, asshole."

"What have you done?

"Now you will find out the price of spying on me," Tucker said and hung up.

Neither Katt nor Gary could speak right away.

Tears were flowing down Katt's cheeks. "That poor kid. She just wanted to do the right thing."

Gary added the latest recording to the growing Tucker file and called Lou Wagner.

"Lou, we think Tucker has killed our mole."

"Aw, Christ. How'd you find out?"

"He called. Didn't mention her by name and didn't say she's dead, but he did refer to our spying on him. I recorded the conversation. There are some other calls, too."

"I want to hear them."

"I'll send you the files."

When he hung up, Gary emailed all of the audios he had been collecting.

"Now Lou will know about the money," Gary said. "But he won't bring it up unless we do."

TWENTY-FOUR

The News Seven receptionist had left a message for them to call Gus.

"What's The Shadow been up to?" Gary said as he hit speed dial.

"*Hola Superman. I couldn't get you on your cell phone so I called the station.*"

"I turned the cell off and forgot to turn it back on. We were trying to sneak around in the woods."

"*What happened in the woods?*"

"A run-in with Tucker's men that ended badly."

"*You guys okay?*"

"Yeah, the other side didn't do well, but I shouldn't talk about it on the phone."

"*Maybe this'll cheer you up.*"

"You have good news?"

"*I found an old police report about the elder Tuckers' fatal crash.*"

"Ancient history."

"*Maybe not. One of the witnesses to the crash said he heard a 'pop' before their car veered off and hit a big rig.*"

"How's that good news?"

"*The report said the police figured Tucker Senior fell asleep. But I know a little about auto mechanics and a 'pop' ain't natural.*"

"You think it was mechanical failure that caused the accident?"

"*Suppose it wasn't an accident.*"

"... and who would benefit if Alex's parents died?"

"*There's something else. The article said they died without a will. What rich businessman doesn't have a will?*"

"They would have been relatively young. Maybe they thought they had plenty of time."

"*Suppose they did have a will and it was never found.*"

"Why would you suspect that?"

"*Because one of Tucker's lawyers' specialty was wills.*"

Gary looked his teammates.

"Without a will the state gets involved and makes the decisions." Katt said. Ties things up for awhile."

"Alex, being the closest relative and a legal adult, would be the heir and get the loot."

"Bingo."

"We need to talk to that lawyer," Jerry said.

"Talk loud, bro, because he died the day after Alex's parents 'accident'."

"Do you know how he died?"

"Funny you should ask because I do know. The day after the Tuckers died he was killed in a hit and run 'accident' as he crossed the street in front of his office."

"Dead men tell no tales," Gary said.

"I wonder if any of the lawyer's files still exist." Katt said.

"I wonder if the death car still exists," Gary said.

"Now you're thinking, amigo. The cops ruled it an accident, but you know how that goes."

"You're a genius, Gus."

"Hell yes."

"Where would the car be if it didn't get sent off to be compacted and melted down?"

"How about to a scrap yard owned by . . . guess who? Alex Tucker?

"My friend, I think you have just given us a really big homework assignment."

"The questions will be on the final."

"Your place isn't gonna be big enough to hold all the cases of Dos Equis we owe you.

"Believe me, I will make room. Adios."

Gary called Lou.

"Now what?"

"How hard would it be to get a warrant to examine the car Alex Tucker's parents died in if it still exists?"

"Why would you want to?"

"It has come to our attention that a witness to the *'accident'*."

"Did I just hear air quotes?"

"You did. What if the witness heard a noise that should not have been there just before the crash?"

"The investigators would have caught that. Maybe."

"But suppose they didn't make anything of it and suppose that car was rusting away in a scrap yard owned by Alex Tucker?"

"If the wreckage even exists after twenty years."

"One way to find out."

To answer your original question, no, there is not enough evidence to get a judge to issue a warrant."

"Well then, how about if the senior Tuckers died without a will, but maybe they didn't?"

"What makes you say that?"

"Because one of their attorneys, who happened to specialize in wills, was run down in the street the day after the Tuckers bought the farm."

"Hmm."

"Hmm, indeed."

"Makes one wonder, but still not enough for a warrant. And do the lawyer's files even exist anymore? Those also were twenty years ago."

"If we could use some of what we've got to get a warrant to search Alex's properties, including his office and residence, it's possible a will could turn up."

"What exactly do we got?"

"Toxic materials dumped in land scheduled for residential development."

"And how did we obtain that information?"

"We took samples from the dump site."

"From private property owned by Alex Tucker."

"Taken by the guy who had been hired to do the dumping."

"Who, while no longer in the employ of Mr. Tucker, also trespassed on private property to obtain the allegedly contaminated material. You see where I'm going with this?"

"That's it for you. No free beer on poker nights."

"Hey, I'm as anxious to nail this guy as you are. But we got rules which, I am historically aware, you never much liked or played by."

"The guy is guilty. We have to stop him."

"No judge would let us go fishing because we have a hunch. Especially in a city where judges are elected and depend on political contributions from Mr. Moneybags."

"We have witnesses that men working for Tucker have abused and intimidated people working against their boss's interests."

"Okay, we could get something on those guys—that guy—since you eliminated one of them. Maybe we could get him to roll over on Tucker if he's still alive."

"Now you're talking. That's the bold, creative, resourceful, aggressive investigator I know."

"And 'handsome'."

"Don't push it."

"I'll see what I can boldly, aggressively, resourcefully create and I'll get back to you."

Wagner clicked off and the team did a round of high pinkies.

An hour later, Lou Wagner called back.

"Got an idea."

"Did it hurt?" Gary said.

"You should be nice to me."

"Why start now?"

In fact, after so many years of busting each others' chops, it would be hard to stop.

"What's your idea?"

"An anonymous party has suggested that the case of the deaths of the elder Tuckers may not have been an accident and urged that the case be reopened. If there are irregularities it would call into question who would inherit their life insurance and properties. In short, who may have had a hand in causing the 'accident'. Did you hear the air quotes?"

"I did. That's thin, but I'll take it."

"The investigating cops can make the decision to reopen. Don't need a judge or a D.A."

"Yeah? What's your next move?"

"Accident investigators are being alerted as we speak. No warrant is necessary since it is a case their department had been

working on that has been reopened. Should any tampering be found, the beneficiaries of the senior Tuckers' estate would be the first place they would look."

"Thus, a warrant. Maybe."

"Maybe."

"Good work you bold, aggressive, resourceful, creative detective.

"You forgot 'handsome'."

"No I didn't," Gary said and hung up.

<u>TWENTY-FIVE</u>

They had promised the station manager they would turn in an occasional feature story to keep the TV audience from wondering whatever happened to the city's most popular reporter.

Team Jerry learned about a twelve-year-old black boy who collected used shoes. He would clean and polish them and then find poor and homeless who needed them. They decided it would make a good feature for the News Seven evening newscasts and found the boy.

"What gave you the idea, Tyrone?" Jerry said.

"Poor people don't have no money for food, let alone good shoes," young Tyrone Libby said. "They go walkin' around in raggedy old shoes and don't feel good about theirselves. Somebody have nice shoes, they got some pride. Ain't a lot pride 'round here."

Gary got some B roll of Tyrone cleaning and polishing shoes and giving them to the needy.

Jerry made three endings to his standup for a variety of purposes. One was the standard outro for the local broadcast. Another was a plea to the TV audience to donate any unused shoes for Tyrone's project and drop them off at a fire station in the boy's neighborhood if they were able to make arrangements after shooting the piece, which they did. A third was for the network if they decided to pick up the story.

These were the kinds of stories Team Jerry had always wanted to do, but could never get them past the former assignment editor. That editor got fired once management realized she didn't actually do anything except take news releases from politicians and public relations agencies and issue assignments based on them. Management decided news people should be looking for stories that affect the viewers, not accepting everything that came in the mail.

"That ought to make Weaver happy," Katt said.

"I expect this story will go national," Jerry said.

But their main focus was to put Alex Tucker out of business.

Next stop, the law offices of Kline, Mohler, and Pearce.

"Twenty years is a long time to keep files," Jerry said.

"Like Lou said, they may have sent them to the client," Gary said. "If Alex got them, you can be sure they were shredded long ago. Still, worth checking out."

The law firm of Kline, Mohler, and Pearce was not located in the high rent district with the city's top law firms. Their office was in a somewhat less prestigious neighborhood.

Gary held the door for Katt. The handicap ramp mandated by the Americans with Disabilities Act gave Jerry easy entry. The inner-office door had a pebbled glass window of the type not seen since the 1930s. Raymond Chandler's Phillip Marlowe would fit right in.

"Someone in there should have a pint bottle of whiskey in a bottom desk drawer," Gary said.

When they entered the office it became obvious they would be dealing with older lawyers. The dark paneling and dim, outdated lighting were typical of a much earlier time. Sounds echoed off the high tin-tiled ceiling and walls lined with shelves filled with law books. Most modern law offices had gone to computerized law 'books' that could quickly be updated when changes were made.

"May I help you?" an elderly receptionist said. A name plate on her desk said 'Rose Sherman'.

"Yes," Katt said. "We are from TV News Seven and wondered if Alex Tucker was one of your clients."

The woman made a sour face and said, "No, we are too old school for the likes of Mr. Tucker. His parents were clients. When they died, the young man switched firms."

"Are there any attorneys still here who handled the elder Tucker account?" Katt said.

"All of the original partners have long since passed," Rose Sherman said. "In fact, one had passed just after the Tuckers died. Bert Levy may be able to help you. Wait here and I'll see if he can talk with you."

The firm lacked an intercom system. She went to one of the offices in the back, her footsteps echoing as she walked.

"I bet Rose was here when the office opened," Katt said quietly.

"I bet Rose was here when dinosaurs roamed these parts," Gary said.

"Why do all law offices smell the same?" Jerry said.

"It's the odor of old paper and billable hours," Gary said. "An aroma not found anywhere else."

The receptionist returned with a slow-moving elderly, gray-haired man who wore a tweed jacket and a vest with a pocket watch on a chain. He had half-glasses that were resting on the bridge of his nose. A bygone era personified.

They introduced themselves and were invited to join the old man in his office.

"Rose said you were inquiring about the Tuckers," Levy said, gesturing for them to be seated.

"More precisely, the parents of Alex Tucker," Jerry said. "We are doing an investigation of the circumstances of their deaths."

The old man looked a little confused. "They died in a terrible traffic accident."

"Well, we have come upon some information that questions whether it actually was an accident."

The old man's jaw dropped.

"My goodness. That could have some far-reaching effects, if true."

"Exactly," Jerry said. "And that is why were wondering whether some of their Tucker files might still exist."

Levy rubbed his chin and seemed to be in deep thought.

Katt was afraid his silence meant the file was gone.

Levy said, "We never destroy documents."

Katt's face lit up.

"Where are those files now?" Jerry asked.

"They would be in boxes in our storage facility."

"Is there any possibility that we could see them?"

"Certainly not without a court order," Levy said. "I'm sure, given the nature of what you said about their deaths perhaps not being accidental, we would be happy to cooperate with the courts. But there still exist confidentially issues."

"Mr. Levy," Katt said. "Could we confide something in you?"

"That is what we do here, Ms Li. Confidentiality is key to an attorney's work. However, you are not a client, so I would have no obligation to keep what is said between us in confidence."

"Suppose I became a client. Would that change things?"

"Of course," Levy said. "For a modest retainer, I could become an ironclad confidant."

Katt reached into a pocket and came out with a five dollar bill.

"Is that modest enough?" she said.

"That should be sufficient," Levy said, pocketing the bill. "Now what did you want to tell me."

"We believe Alex Tucker murdered his parents."

The shock that registered on Bert Levy's face was somewhere between flabbergasted and gob smacked.

"Dear God, do you realize what you're saying?"

"We do. And we have more than enough reason to believe it is true. What we lack is solid proof."

"How can this firm help?"

"At the time of their deaths, a news report said the senior Tuckers died intestate. That is really hard to believe. If they actually did have a will and a copy exists in those files, it could provide information about their intended beneficiaries."

"There certainly should have been a will, although I did not handle their legal work. One of our deceased senior partners did."

"If someone wanted any information about a Tucker will covered up, wouldn't it be convenient for the lawyer who handled that to have a fatal hit-and-run accident?"

Levy sat back in his chair, speechless. Finally he said, "That would shed an entirely new light on the Tucker estate and on young Mr. Tucker in particular."

"What if there were others who were intended to benefit and the son found that inconvenient?" Katt said. "You have to understand that Alex Tucker is nothing like his public image. He is a cruel, manipulating man who gets his way by whatever means necessary. We believe he is guilty of the murders of his parents personally and he has hired others to do his killing for him."

Levy again sank into deep thought. Katt, Gary, and Jerry stayed quiet, letting him come to his own conclusions.

"Here is what I can do," Levy said finally. "I can go through those files to see if there was a will. If there was, and if I determine there is any reason there might exist a motive for murder, I would be obligated to inform the authorities of that fact."

"That's great," Katt said. "If and when that happens, would you contact Carsonville Police Detective Lou Wagner? He has been working with us on this case."

Katt gave the lawyer Lou's direct contact information, thanked him and left the old attorney to think about what they had told him. And to consider the likelihood that one of the law firm's own partners may have been murdered.

Gary called Lou and let him know what to expect.

"What if there is no will?"

"Then we're back to where we started," Gary said. "It was worth a shot. Right now Alex is really nervous. people make mistakes."

"Desperate people also sometimes resort to violence."

"He's already done that, so it's a given."

"He is also smart, and he has resources."

"Even if we stopped our investigation right now, Alex is coming for us. Our only choice is to keep on doing what we've been doing."

"I'll let you know if I hear from Levy."

Jerry's cell phone rang. Cheryl calling.

"Hi. Everything okay?"

"All is well. I missed talking with you."

"I miss you, too."

"Is this ever going to be over?"

"Soon, I hope. We seem to be making some progress."

"This is no way to live."

"Is Janet there with you?"

"Yes. I couldn't ask for better protection."

"Can I talk to her?"

Jerry could hear Cheryl calling for her favorite bodyguard.

"What's up, sport?"

"I didn't want to mention this to Cheryl, but Gary and another guy we're working with got into a gun battle with those two Tucker thugs. One dead, the other wounded, but got away."

"There are plenty more mercs for hire out there."

"That's what we've been told. Tucker is in a corner and you know what happens when rats are cornered. Anyway, I wanted to update you and didn't want to worry Cheryl."

"A great girl that Cheryl. Too good for you, of course."

"I know that, for sure. Take care of her. And take care of yourself while you're at it."

"Ten-four."

Cheryl came back on.

"You two keeping secrets?"

"Just letting her know that Tucker's getting desperate and to be extra alert. You're safe, but we aren't taking any chances."

"Come for dinner and bring Katt and Gary."

Jerry turned and said, "We're invited to dinner at Cheryl's fortress."

"We'll have to make it another time," Katt said. "Gary and I have a couple of things we have to do."

"It's a standing invitation. But you can come, Jerry."

"I'll be there."

"See you at seven. Or before. Or now. Bye."

"I'll check your car again for trackers," Gary said. "Didn't find one, but you should still drive around town for awhile to be sure you don't have a tail."

Katt and Gary did not really have anything else to do. They just thought the lovebirds would like some time alone.

TWENTY-SIX

How was dinner at Cheryl's last night?" Katt said.

"Wonderful. So was the food. What's on the work menu?"

"We have to find out why we haven't heard anything about Alice Simms?" Katt said.

"Tucker's going to want us to know she's dead," Gary said. "He won't bury her. He will have her where she can be found."

Jerry said, "We should check with the morgue."

"I hope she's alive and healthy," Katt said. "But I know that's wishful thinking."

"Tucker already as much as told us he had her killed."

"I've got the number for the morgue."

A dark mood had fallen over the editing booth. Fear that Tucker's words about them "spying" on him meant he had disposed of the young intern was bad enough. Not really knowing what may have happened was taking a toll on them.

Katt clicked off her phone and looked like someone who had received bad news.

"What?" Gary said.

"They have a Jane Doe," Katt said. "Hit and run victim. I made an appointment."

"That would be Tucker's go-to murder method," Jerry said.

Katt moved toward the door. "I'll go," she said. "You didn't know her."

"We should all go," Jerry said. "If she died for the cause, we can at least pay our respects."

In most cities, morgues were in basements of buildings. But, because of occasional earth tremors that could put cracks in building foundations and result in water seepage, basements were a rarity in California. Carsonville's morgue was located on the top floor of a building in the warehouse district, far from view of residents sheltered from the darker side of city life.

The elevator to the upper floors was a large, no-frills affair designed to accommodate gurneys transporting bodies as well as employees and those who had come to identify the dead. .

The atmosphere inside was cold in mood and temperature. The smell hit them before they had even entered the area where autopsies were performed.

"Ugh," Katt said. "How can people work here?"

"You get used to it, I guess," Gary said.

"Who would choose this as a profession?" Jerry said.

"Ghouls who went to college would be my guess," Katt said.

That image was quickly dispelled when the head man introduced himself. He looked like someone's friendly uncle rather than a person who cut up corpses for a living.

"Good morning," he said. "I'm Coroner Ed Higgins. "The Jane Doe I mentioned on the phone was a hit-and-run victim. She had no identification on her, so we couldn't locate any relatives."

"Fingerprints didn't tell you anything?" Katt said.

"Nothing. You would be surprised at how many people have no fingerprint records; never arrested or applied for a government job or served in the military. Some parents have the right idea, getting their children fingerprinted in case they are ever kidnapped. Those prints won't change and they will be on file all their lives. Our victim was one of those not on record.

"As I understand it, she was found along a rural road with no purse or wallet or other form of identification. Broken glasses presumed to be hers were found some distance from the body. She had been hit at high speed and the driver left her there. I'm sure there was a lot of damage to the vehicle, as well."

The room where refrigerated units lined one wall was brightly lighted to give pathologists a better view of their work at the tables spread out in front of a wall of cooling units.

Higgins led them to a bank of steel doors, each about four-feet by four-feet with handles similar to those on home refrigerators. He opened one. Inside was a small body covered from head to toe with a sheet. He pulled on the drawer and slid it into the room.

The four of them gathered around as Higgins gently removed the sheet from the victim's face.

An intake of breath from Katt.

The young woman looked very small, almost child-like. Bruises and abrasions were evident. They could only imagine what trauma the rest of her body had suffered.

Tears flowed down Katt's cheeks. With great difficulty she said, "That is Alice Simms."

"What can you tell me about her?" Higgins said as he covered the victim. He slid the drawer back into its compartment and closed the door.

"I don't know much about her," Katt struggled to say. "She was an intern for the Tucker Development Corporation. I only met her on two occasions. We never discussed family."

"Do you have any suggestions about how we should handle the remains?" Higgins said.

"If you could contact a funeral home," Gary said, "We will take care of the costs."

Higgins nodded. "If you give me your phone number and an email address I can send you the details."

No one spoke on the elevator on the way to the ground floor.

Katt was still choked up in the van. "That poor kid. She knew what could happen and she was willing to work with us anyway. She told me she wasn't a brave person."

"She was wrong about that," Jerry said. "She was the bravest person I've ever heard of. I'm sorry I never met her."

"What was she doing on a rural road?" Katt said.

"My guess," Gary said, "is that one of the Tucker new hires drove her there, let her out on to road and told her to walk back to the city, then turned around and ran her down."

They went back to the TV station to brainstorm what to do next.

"I want Alex Tucker to die for this," Gary said. "Or sent to prison for life without a chance of parole."

"Life in prison could be worse than death," Jerry said. "Especially for someone who has lived the privileged life he has."

"Katt said, "No. He has to die. And not just quietly go to sleep forever on a gurney in San Quentin's execution chamber. He has to die as painfully and as slowly as possible."

"Is there something wrong with us that we would want that for someone?" Jerry said.

"I think there would be something wrong with us if we didn't," Gary said.

Katt checked her phone for messages and emails, which she had been neglecting lately with all that was going on. One was a voice mail from two days earlier from an unidentified caller. Where she might normally have deleted the caller as spam, she decided to listen to it.

As she pushed the 'play' button, Katt had a look of horror on her face. She broke down in sobs. When she gained some control she put the voice message on speaker.

"Ms Li, this is Alice Simms. I'm calling from home. I just wanted to let you know that I overheard Mr. Tucker talking with two men. They're not the same ones as before, but they're the same type. He said 'I don't care how you do it, but I want those TV people dead'. He also said to 'find the girlfriend and take care of her'. I don't know if they noticed me at the copy machine, but he shut the door to his office right after that. I will keep looking for files that show anything suspicious and get back to you then. I'm a little scared. Anyway, I will talk to you when I have something."

Katt was sitting with her head in her hands.

"If I had listened to my voice mail when it came in we could have saved that poor kid. We could have pulled her out of there."

Nothing Jerry or Gary could have said at that moment would have helped, so they each put a hand on a shoulder and held it there until she stopped sobbing."

"I need to destroy him," she said. "I'm about ready to go bat shit. Just march into his office and ruin his day."

"You would die in the effort," Gary said. "We will get Tucker, but we will do it in a way that causes the most damage to his little empire and to him personally."

<u>TWENTY-SEVEN</u>

It took only a glance for Katt to size up the manager of the salvage yard as the type that a hundred-dollar bill would get answers to some questions and not ask any of his own.

"You can't let my boss know about this," Charlie McMillan said. "I could lose my job."

"I absolutely promise I won't say a word."

What the man didn't know was that telling Tucker of her visit could only get him fired. It could get her killed.

Katt wanted to have a look around among the hundreds of cars and trucks waiting to be stripped of parts or placed into a giant compressing machine and turned into cubes of steel. Those would be shipped off to a steel mill to be melted and become girders, sheet metal, and even more cars and trucks.

"Where do you get your cars?" Katt said.

"Get 'em all kind of ways," McMillan said. "Some are donated to raise money for charities. People often give their old wrecks to non-profits and take a tax deduction. Some of 'em come from places like farms where they were sitting and rusting away."

"I'll bet you have a lot of cars that had been in accidents," Katt said.

"Them too."

"You compress them and ship them out for scrap?"

"Once they've been robbed of usable parts, out they go."

"So, there wouldn't be any that have been here for very long?"

"Depends on what you mean by very long," McMillan said.

"I mean years and years."

"Well, we got one been here for, maybe, twenty years or so."

"Why would you keep one that long?"

"Cause the owner of this place ordered us not to sell any parts off it or junk it."

Katt felt a wave of excitement, but didn't want to show it.

"But it's not good for anything but parts and scrap metal. Why would anyone want to keep it?"

"This one, his parents died in it. He kinda made it like a shrine. Comes by once in awhile just to look at it. Remembering his folks, I guess."

Probably admiring his handiwork.

"Could I see it?"

"Don't see why not if you keep it between me and you."

"Absolutely."

The manager led Katt through a jungle of junked vehicles to a spot that was sparsely populated with wrecks. A lone Mercedes sat with flat tires, twisted steering, a completely destroyed front end, the engine resting in the passenger compartment. Weeds grew all around it, some rising up through the engine compartment and pushing through the hood.

"I guess you get accident vehicles all the time."

"Two in the past couple of weeks. One was a fatal on Highway 50. Another one, the owner hit a deer."

Katt's surprised look was not that a deer could total a car, but that it might not have been a deer.

"How can hitting a deer make a car a candidate for the scrap heap?" she said.

"Oh, man, you hit a deer at high speed and it can do a lot of damage. The guy who brought it in said repairs would cost more than the car was worth. Couldn't drive it around with one headlight hanging down, and pieces of chrome about to drop off. So he brought it here. I gave him fifty bucks for it."

"Can I see it?"

"Sure, it's right over there," McMillan said, pointing to an older model Ford with a badly damaged front end.

Katt moved closer to the car. It was plain to see blood on the grill and hood. She could not hold back the tears.

"You okay, Miss?"

"That poor deer," she said.

"Sometimes you can't help hitting them. They run right across the road in front of you. You slam 100-pounds of meat and bones into a car at high speed and that's what you get. This driver was lucky he didn't die. He was a big man. It'd take a lot to kill a guy as big as him."

We'll see about that.

The idea that innocent Alice Simms was reduced to "meat and bones" enraged Katt.

"There sure are a lot of cars here," Katt said, pointing down the row of scrapped vehicles.

When McMillan turned away for a second, Katt took a tissue and swiped it across an area stained with blood and quickly put it in a pocket.

Katt asked to see several other cars before wrapping up her tour. She didn't want the manager to think she was only interested in the Tucker car and the one she was all but certain was the car that hit Alice Simms.

"Well, thanks for showing me around," Katt said, and left the yard.

Back in her car she called Gary to report what she had learned.

"It's the one that hit Alice, I'm sure."

"We'll need proof."

"I took a sample of the blood on the grill."

"I'll see what Lou wants to do about it."

"I'm headed for the station after I stop at the morgue."

Gary wasted no time calling Lou Wagner.

"Speak to me."

"Katt found the Tucker death car."

"That's a start."

"And, Lou, she found a car she thinks is the one used to hit our mole, Alice Simms."

"Thinking it and proving it are two different matters."

"She took a sample of blood that was on the grill."

"Even if it turns out to be the victim's blood, the sample was taken without a warrant."

"Yes, but we'd know for sure. Plus, there would be the driver's fingerprints in the car to tie him to Alice Simms and to Tucker."

"Let me get with the D.A. and see how we might handle this. Meanwhile, let's get that blood sample compared with the victim's for a possible DNA match."

The district attorney was a friend of Katt and Gary's. Susan Griffin had been a deputy D.A. when she nearly died in a hit-and-run attack for helping them with their investigation of the Russian mob. One of the would-be assassins tried a second time to kill her in her hospital bed as Gary was standing guard. He and Katt had become her friends and protectors. Susan was hailed a hero for her actions. She became so popular with the public for her bravery that when a special election was held she ran for the District Attorney's office she won by a record majority of the vote.

Susan Griffin was incorruptible and absolutely immune to any of Alex Tucker's influence.

"Why don't *I* call her, Lou?"

"That's right. You guys have a history. Yeah, you call and see what you can work out."

Gary had Susan's private number. She answered right away.

"Gary. It's been awhile."

"Too long, Susan. Being busy is no excuse."

"I'm glad you and Katt finally figured it out and got together. I love her like a sister."

"It's mutual. Are your injuries all healed?"

"I will always have a slight limp. The hip never got lined up quite right and I have some arthritis. Otherwise I'm back to normal."

Gary explained about their investigation of Alex Tucker and what evidence they had. He told her of the murder of their mole, the attacks on themselves and a friend. He even confessed to the gunfight on Tucker property.

"There also could be a will, although it didn't turn up when the senior Tuckers died, murdered by their own son. And Alex inherited the whole bundle as the result. The senior Tucker family's law firm is looking into it and you may have to get all legal on him to have a look at a will, if there is one. And, by the way, Junior may also have knocked off the lawyer who did the will work for his parents. That would have been back in the days when he did his own killing instead of paying mercenaries to do it for him."

"Whoa. Okay, there is a lot to digest and there are some holes here. Let's see if we can find ways to work with them. I'll get busy on it, check the legal issues, and map a strategy."

"Can't ask for more than that."

"When things settle down we should all get together and get drunk and disorderly."

"In my wildest imagination I cannot picture Susan Griffin in such a condition, but let's do get together soon."

Gary called Lou again.

"And—?"

"Susan is on board.

"We're gonna nail this guy yet."

"We?"

"You guys helped a little."

"You sound like the FBI. We do the work, you take the credit."

"We'll mention your tiny contribution in our final report."

"What a pal."

"Get that blood sample to the coroner ASAP."

"Katt is stopping there on her way back to the station."

Coroner Edward Higgins accepted the sample Katt had taken and said he would put a rush on it as well as the sample taken from Alice Simms to see if they were a match.

"I don't know how long it will take," Higgins said. "We don't do DNA testing here. We contract with a company in Sacramento."

"The sooner, the better, doc. This is a murder case and the suspect knows we're after him. He could make a run for it."

"I'll mark it a priority."

Katt drove back to the station.

Gary called Lou Wagner.

"Katt dropped off the blood sample. What have you got?"

"An enlarged prostate. What have you got?"

"An urgent need to commit murder."

"Take two aspirin and call me in the morning."

"Okay, besides that."

"Got a call from Attorney Bert Levy."

"Good news, I hope."

"It's the start of good news. Getting to that news may take some doing."

"I think you're saying there is a will and you have to find a way."

"Yep."

"But he can't divulge the contents without a warrant."

"Yep, Part Two."

"You'd better be the one to call Susan this time."

"Already got a call in."

"It feels like progress, but I don't want to jinx it by getting too worked up."

"If we can prove any one of the things we know it'll be like dominos falling. One warrant can give us something else that will justify another and so on."

"Tinker to Evers to Chance," Gary said, referring to a poem about an historic double play in a 1910 baseball game between the New York Yankees and Chicago Cubs.

"For the out that won the World Series."

TWENTY-EIGHT

The coroner says DNA results could come back in as little as two or three days," Katt said. "That's if the lab gets to it right away. They're usually pretty busy."

"So, we wait," Jerry said.

Jerry was also waiting for his carry permit, having completed the required training and application process.

"You're not legal yet, Jer," Gary said. "But you have to be armed now."

"I'm a lawbreaker trying to catch a lawbreaker. There's some irony in there somewhere."

Gary's cell phone rang.

"Yeah, Lou."

"Okay, so we know there was a will."

"Does Susan know?"

"She's on it. She's gonna try to sell it to a judge."

"An elected judge who takes Tucker campaign money?" Gary said. "Lotsa luck."

"Patience, my friend."

"It's not something I am well known for."

"Don't I know it?" Wagner said and hung up.

"The funeral home called," Katt said, the dark sadness had returned. "Alice Simms can be ready for burial in a day or so."

Katt continued to blame herself for the young woman's death. Nothing Gary or Jerry had said did anything to comfort her.

"If it helps," Jerry said, "I was the one who said we should have a mole in Tucker's office."

"It doesn't help, Jerry," Katt said, giving Jerry a little side hug. "But thanks for trying."

"While we're waiting for a warrant we should do a feature to keep the GM happy," Gary said.

"How about a follow-up to the kid who gives shoes away?" Jerry said. "The fire station is getting a lot of donations."

"Let's go," Katt said, and they headed out.

Team Jerry had their camera equipment set up for the interview.

"With me is Fire Captain Bryan Elliott." Jerry said. "He and his fellow firefighters have volunteered to take in donations of used shoes for young Tyrone Libby. This after a story News Seven did about the young man's rehabbing shoes and giving them to the poor and needy in the community. Captain, how's the donation program going?"

"Almost too good."

"Really?"

"We've been overwhelmed with donated shoes and we're running out of space in the station to store them."

"Kind of a good position to be in, wouldn't you say?"

"Absolutely. We'll find space somewhere. The young man saw the need and didn't wait around for someone else to solve the problem. He did it. He does odd jobs to make money to buy polish and other supplies. Tyrone Libby is a genuine hero."

Even as the interview was underway, more donors had come in with shoes. Gary got B roll of them.

"Nice that the public has been so generous," Jerry said.

"Tyrone made a good argument for the need."

No sooner had Elliott mentioned Tyrone than the boy arrived at the fire station pulling a beat up express wagon. It was rusted and the rubber tire had fallen off one rim.

Gary turned his camera on the boy.

"You're gonna need a bigger wagon, Tyrone," Elliott said. "We have lots of shoes for you and we can bring them to your house for you. In fact, how about if we bring you a brand new wagon?"

Gary was getting it all on video.

Jerry asked him a few questions on camera, then wrapped up the piece, again doing separate outros in case the network wanted the feature.

"I didn't want to say anything in the interview," Elliott said. "But there have been a lot of cash donations, too. Over nine-hundred dollars so far. But if word got out that the kid had that kind of money, he would be in danger. We'll open a bank account and give him the cash on the sly as he needs it. His family is really desperate."

"I'll bet he'll spend most of it on poor people," Katt said.

"Wouldn't be surprised," Elliott said.

Their work done, they loaded the van and started back to the TV station to put the piece together for the evening newscast.

They were only a few minutes into the drive to the station when Gary alerted.

"Don't look," Gary said, "but we've got a tail. A Dodge van." He jacked a cartridge into the camber of the new Colt 45 and sat it on the seat where he could reach it. He rolled the driver's side window down.

Jerry readied Janet's 1911. He rolled down his window, as well.

"I see two heads," Gary said. "Alex must have hired more muscle. Get down, Katt."

Katt slid down onto the passenger side floor.

After several blocks, the van suddenly accelerated and pulled up beside Gary's van.

When the vehicle was exactly even with them, the side door slid open and a man with a handgun aimed it at Gary.

"Gary fired two shots. Jerry fired two. The combination of hits propelled the gunman backwards. Seeing his man down, the driver dropped back and turned into the next street.

"Good one, Jerry," Gary said. "I don't think they were expecting that."

Jerry was shaken. Until that moment he had only fired the gun at paper targets. Never at a person.

"I know I hit him," Jerry said.

"We both did."

Gary called Lou.

"Yeah?"

"Two thugs in a van just tried to kill us as we were driving back from doing a story," Gary said."

"You don't seem to be killed. What happened?"

"We hit the shooter and sent him flying."

"We?"

"I mean I shot him."

"You got Jerry a gun, didn't you? I know Katt doesn't use one."

"Yeah. Jerry went through the training program for certification. Hasn't received the carry permit in the mail yet."

"I'm not crazy about civilians flinging lead around on city streets."

"I was watching background, Lou. It was clear. There was no other choice. If we hadn't been armed, we wouldn't be having this conversation."

"Yeah, I get that."

"Something else," Gary said. "Neither the shooter nor the driver were the original hit squad members. Maybe the survivor we hit at our shootout on the Sierra Estates property is recovering somewhere."

"Or dead somewhere. I've been thinking about that. Tucker wouldn't want cops questioning him in a hospital about gunshot wounds."

"So, rather than patch him up, you think they may have finished him off."

"That'd be my guess."

"Whatever happened to employer loyalty? Stay in touch."

Jerry had been pretty quiet since the shooting.

"You okay, Jer?"

"I don't think I'll ever be okay."

Gary knew from experience that taking a life is hard, especially the first time, even if that person deserved to die. It left a scar on the one who took it. Nothing he could say to Jerry right now could ease his pain.

"Talk to us, Jer," Katt said.

Jerry didn't say anything right away. When he did, he was very quiet.

"I caused the death of another person."

Katt put a hand on Jerry's shoulder and gave it a light squeeze.

"All I can say, Jer, is that time will ease the pain."

Jerry stayed quiet. Gary and Katt knew that the best thing they could do for their friend was to be there for him.

"We got the warrant, Gary."

"I heard, Susan. Any problem with the judge?"

"None. Old Judge Harlan Wilcox is retiring after this term, so he doesn't need Alex Tucker's campaign money. But I think he would have issued it anyway. He said he would give us a second warrant for Tucker's home and office if we find evidence of motive. I'm headed for the lawyer's office."

"When will Team Jerry get a look at the will?"

"You can go there with us right now."

"I'll call Lou . . ."

"I already did. He'll meet us."

They drove straight to the office of the dead lawyers, Kline, Mohler, and Pearce.

Receptionist Rose Sherman led them to the conference room.

Spread out on the long dark walnut table were dozens of papers yellowed with age. Susan and Lou were looking over them.

Susan said, "the will clearly shows the elder Tuckers intended to leave a large portion of their estate to various charitable and cultural organizations and a pittance to their son."

"I don't think they liked little Alex," Gary said.

"They aren't the only ones," Katt said.

"I don't understand how the man can have such a positive public image," Susan said, "with such a sinister background."

"People see what they want to see and the rich usually get a pass," Jerry said. "Watch how quickly the public turns on him when this gets out."

Bert Levy picked up a notebook from the mass of papers on the table and said, "These are notes taken by the partner who handled the account. There are some sharp comments in there which, of course, he would not have shared with the Tuckers. He wondered why they would practically abandon their son. Naturally, all we can do is to follow the dictates of the client."

Susan packed up the material in her briefcase and snapped it shut.

"I'll stop by the judge's chamber and pick up the new warrant," Susan said. "We can serve it in the morning."

"It could be dangerous," Gary said. Lou and Hank agreed.

They all knew that serving the papers on Tucker might meet armed resistance.

"We'll be dressed for the occasion," Wagner said.

Jerry called Cheryl.

"I hadn't heard from you in awhile and I was starting to worry."

"Well, I've been thinking about you. We've been pretty tied up with this Tucker investigation. It looks like the danger may soon come to an end."

"That's good news. Can I finally get rid of Janet and Frank?" She giggled.

Jerry could hear Janet in the background.

"Gimme that phone," Janet said. *"What makes you think Cheryl can get rid of us?"*

"Because Alex Tucker is just about finished."

"Well, sport, Frank and I ain't leaving until Tucker is in chains or dead. We're staying even if we don't get paid. We like this kid."

"I like your attitude, Janet. We're working on the project. Let me talk to the kid again."

"Even after this is over I'm keeping them." Cheryl said.

"Friends forever, as far as I'm concerned. I will see you very soon."

TWENTY-NINE

Gary and Katt dropped Gary's van off with a company that installs wheelchair lifts. They would use the satellite van until the installation was finished.

Carsonville police officers and detectives who were part of Lou Wagner's trusted core group stood guard at Alex Tucker's home and office, just in case he tried to run for it.

First on the list was Tucker's office.

District Attorney Susan Griffin was accompanied by two of her deputies and several armed and armored cops. Susan and her aides also wore bullet resistant vests as she, Lou, Hank, and Team Jerry with their camera gear came out of the elevator and into the reception area.

With no warning, the group walked past a protesting receptionist.

"We have a search warrant," Susan said, waving the paper at the woman.

The door to the inner offices would not open,

"Buzz us in," Susan told the receptionist.

"You can't go in there without being announced," She said and pushed a button under her desk.

There was no buzz.

"Did you just send a warning?" Susan said. "That may very well cost you your freedom."

One of the officers pushed her aside and found the release button that let the group inside.

Tucker's so-called Chief of Staff, Kathy Rankin, was waiting for them.

"Where is Alex Tucker?" Susan said.

"You must leave right now," Rankin said. "You have no right to barge in here like this."

Susan shoved a copy of the search warrant into her hands and pushed her out of the way.

All she got from the rest of the staff were wide-eyed looks and shrugs.

"Everyone to the reception area," Susan said. She instructed officers to block the elevator and hold them there until the search was completed. Nobody out, nobody in.

Tucker's office was empty. A video monitor at his desk showed images from several angles in reception.

"He saw us coming," Lou said.

"The receptionist warned him and he got away," Jerry said.

They could hear the sound of an engine coming from above them.

As the D.A.'s staffers rummaged through desks and computers, Gary noticed a bookcase in Tucker's private office that had a semi-circle indentation in the carpet in front of it

"This bookcase is a door," Gary said. "See, it swings out."

He felt around for a latch, found it, and eased the bookcase back to reveal a stairway to the roof.

"There's a heliport up there," Lou said.

The engine sound faded as Gary charged up the steps.

"He's gone," Lou called after him. "Not important for now."

Gary came back down to Tucker's office.

"We can't get into the computers." Susan said.

"Huh? Oh, right," Gary said and took out his phone and made a call.

"Shadowman, would you open Tucker's files please?"

"That would be illegal, senor."

"It certainly would."

"All the more fun. Give me one sec, mi amigo."

A heartbeat later.

"You got it."

"Try it again, Susan," Gary said.

"We're in," yelled one of the deputies.

"Susan stood, open-mouthed. "How did you do that, Gary?"

"Magic."

The files were opened and downloaded to large-capacity external drives they brought with them.

"Take the processors," Susan told her deputies.

"We won't be able to access Tucker's Local Area Network off-site," Susan said.

"Yes you will," Gary said.

"How? Never mind."

"Magicians never tell how their tricks work." Katt said.

"You guys are really something," Susan said.

"We live to serve," Jerry said.

When the files had been downloaded, Gary got on the phone again.

"Shadowman, would you please lock them up again?"

"My pleasure senor."

"You don't have to call me 'senor', 'Your Majesty' will do."

"This is fun. Someday maybe you'll tell me what the hell we've been doing."

"I'll give you whole story soon, my friend. Got no secrets from you, there just hasn't been time to keep you up on everything. Later, dude."

"You have a very interesting circle of friends, Gary," Susan said. "Shadowman?"

"He works in the shadows. Let me know when you want to get into the LAN. I will wave my wand."

Susan just shook her head and smiled.

The crew packed up everything; computer processors, hard copy, notes, anything that contained data. That done, they adjourned to the reception area.

"Okay," Susan told staffers, "Mr. Tucker is suspected of a long list of crimes. If I learn that any of you aided him in those alleged crimes, you will be prosecuted. My very strong suggestion is that you give no further assistance from this date or you will add to any future charges."

The staff members were released and scurried onto the elevator to get away from the place.

"Ms Rankin, you are free for now, but you should not leave Carsonville. And you might want to think about getting a lawyer."

"I haven't done anything wrong."

"You have aided a criminal. If it can be proven that you knew you were participating in those crimes, you will be arrested and charged."

When everyone was out of hearing range of the staff, Susan said, "On to his home."

Tucker and his thug, who was checked out in the helicopter, barely got away before the police came up the stairs to the roof of Tucker Tower.

Alex Tucker still lived in the house he grew up in. It was a McMansion built many years before anyone heard the term. If he thought he could retreat safely there, police officers stationed at all exits as he flew over the house changed his mind.

"To the mountains," Tucker said. They turned the helicopter around and headed for the Sierra Nevada.

In less than a half hour he and his remaining hired killer arrived at a mountain cabin hideaway.

"We should be okay here," Tucker said.

They off-loaded weapons and supplies. Ever since the TV people started investigating him he kept the helicopter close by. It was filled with things he would need if he had to run. Many people keep a go-bag, Tucker kept a go-chopper. His paranoia had paid off.

They had gotten out of the office with no time to spare, thanks to the receptionist's warning. When he saw armed police in combat gear on the monitors, it didn't take a genius to figure out they were there for him. He and his hired thug made a dash for the secret stairway. There had been barely enough time to warm up the helicopter's engine.

Hank and Lou stood at the front of the Tucker mansion with Team Jerry.

"We'll search Tucker's place and worry about finding him later," Lou said.

"For all practical purposes, Alex is out of business," Hank said. "He can't come back here or he'll be arrested. There's almost nowhere he can go because he can't get to any money he may still have in the bank and he is a wanted man."

"It's just a matter of time," Jerry said. "I just hope no one gets hurt before he gets put away."

"Well then you'd better keep him out of my way," Katt said. "Because if I get my hands on him he's the one gonna get hurt."

Hank smiled. He had no idea that Katt's threat actually had teeth in it.

A ramp led to the front door of the house. Handy for Jerry to keep up with the group.

The door was locked. A battering ram made splinters of it. The entry led to a living room filled with artworks and walls lined with book-filled shelves.

"Do you suppose Alex read all these?" Katt said.

"I'm sure he had people to do that for him," Jerry said.

Tucker had a home office computer. It was confiscated along with a cabinet filled with files. A wall safe behind a painting was beyond the expertise of anyone on the crew to open it, so they simply ripped it from the wall and took it with them.

Then it was on to the District Attorney's office to examine their booty.

The D.A's conference room was filled with computer processors and file boxes. A locksmith worked on opening the confiscated safe. Staffers were combing through the treasure trove. There was an occasional shout to alert Susan that something of value had been discovered.

Gary Mansfield was capturing it all on video.

"Tucker has committed crimes even beyond what we came looking for," Susan said. "Blackmail, gunrunning. I'll put these blackmail materials away. We don't want those to be made public. This warrant only covers whether the suspect had a copy of a will or knowledge of one that allowed him to inherit what he wasn't entitled to. But, if other crimes are discovered during the search I'll have to get back with the judge to see whether the warrant covers it.

"It sure is nice to have a D.A. for a friend," Gary said. "Especially a beautiful one."

"Now, see," Susan said, turning to Katt. "I already want to jump his bones and then he says things like that."

"I know," Katt said. "Frustrating. But what can you do?"

"Aren't you jealous?"

"Heck no. He and I are two peas in a pod. I know he adores you. So do I. Besides, if he stepped out on me he'd end up looking like he went through a smoothie blender."

Gary just smiled, gave Katt a side hug, and leaned down to kiss her on top of her head.

Jerry's professionalism was never more evident in the eyes of his teammates than when he rose above his depression over shooting Tucker's thug. He did a flawless standup on the story of Alex Tucker's fall from grace.

When they returned to the station, Katt, Jerry, and Gary went into the general manager's office.

"I'm proud of you guys," Cyrus Weaver said. "But I'm also afraid for your safety."

"Part of the job," Gary said.

"No it's not," Weaver said. "What other TV field reporting team do you know of that does anything but report the story? Team Jerry is one of a kind, I'm sure."

"Okay then," Gary said, "it's part of the job as we define the job. One of the big failings with TV news reporting has been superficial coverage. The newspapers are dying and with them, investigative reporting. Getting to the heart of stories take time."

"That's where we come in." Katt said. "If we're going to investigate, there is always some risk."

"We appreciate your support," Gary said. "We realize you're taking a career risk by backing us. We will try not to get you in trouble."

"Nothing like the risks you're taking. I've bought into what you're doing, so I'll take what comes. You have demonstrated that you are able to take care of yourselves, but I still worry."

They did not tell him about the most recent shooting incident because they knew he would worry even more. Maybe even insist that they call it off. Not that it would stop them.

"All we can do is stay alert for trouble and avoid it where possible," Jerry said.

They edited the Tucker story for broadcast that evening and turned the package over to the director.

<u>THIRTY</u>

The detectives thought it would be a good idea to assemble all the parties in the D.A's office for a strategy session.

"I can't believe I'm letting a civilian weenie in on this," Wagner said.

"I can't believe I'm letting cops in on this," Gary said. "I have a much less gentle way in mind to handle Mr. Tucker."

Wagner ignored him.

"Don't ignore me in that tone of voice, young man," Gary said.

"Suppose we find the little weasel, Susan," Hank said. "What do we have that could give him more than a slap on the wrist? Or something that would cost him a bundle?"

"There was a copy of the will in that safe we got from his house," Susan said. "He knew who was supposed to get what. We've got him dead-bang on the grand larceny charge. He will serve some prison time and will have to make restitution. There is some question as to whether he can come up with enough."

"I thought he was the 200-million dollar man," Jerry said.

"We think that was something he put out there to impress the public. His wealth is tied up in highly leveraged properties. He would take out a loan on one property and use that money toward the purchase of another one. Rental income was making the payments on the loans. He doesn't even own Tucker Tower outright. If he missed a payment on any of them his house of cards would crumble. Even that would not have been enough to cover the debt, which begs the question: where did the difference come from? We're still digging."

"So he's pretty much a paper millionaire?" Katt said.

"It looks that way. He may be able to put his hands on a couple hundred thousand dollars in cash, but the rest is tied up in a mirage."

"If it all collapsed it would leave him relatively broke," Katt said. "No money for hot shot lawyers, either."

"Maybe you could give him a loan, Katt," Jerry said. "To help him get back on his feet."

"If we still had hanging as capital punishment," Katt said, "that would get him off his feet."

"I'm glad we're on the verge of bankrupting him," Lou said. "And maybe we'll put him in prison for awhile but I was hoping we could get him for murder."

"Baby steps, detective," Susan said. "One thing leads to another, to another, to another. We'll get him. It just won't be today."

What about contractors who are owed money." Katt said.

"Six current, four past, including the dead subcontractors," Susan said. "Nothing we can do about those. Even Alex's employees won't get paid."

Katt looked at Gary and Jerry. Gary nodded.

"Could we get a list of those short-changed subcontractors?" Gary said.

Susan handed Katt the list.

"We're going back to the station," Jerry said.

Instead they sat in Gary's van and surfed the Internet for addresses and phone numbers for the contractors and for the survivors of the murder victims.

While everyone was thinking of punishment for Tucker, Alex Tucker was thinking of ways to punish those who put him in the situation he was in.

Life in a rustic cabin provided the basics, but it was far from what Tucker was accustomed to. Meals out of cans was not at all acceptable to a man who had dined regularly in the finest restaurants in the city. People catered to his every desire. Now he was sharing space with a savage and being denied what he was entitled to.

"I want those TV people dead," Tucker said.

Tucker's mercenary, a man named Robert Shultz, agreed.

"They killed my buddy," Shultz said. "We served together in Special Ops in Afghanistan."

The elite force created some of the best fighters on earth. They were a tough breed of men, some of whom were well suited to the military but not at all to life among civilized people. Shultz and his dead friend were two of that kind.

"They'll be easy to find," Tucker said. "We can wait at the TV station and follow them."

When it started to look like there might be trouble, Tucker's so-called chief of staff, who was also his lover, had planned well for the very situation he found himself in. He wanted to find her and get her away from whatever the police had in mind. She was holding nearly two-hundred-thousand dollars cash Tucker had put aside for this very kind of emergency. In part he wanted to find her because she knew everything about his business and, literally, knew where the bodies were buried.

But first, the TV people.

They would get a good night sleep. In the morning they would go hunting.

THIRTY-ONE

If we can find those people who got screwed," Katt said, "Alex is going to pay them what he owes them. He just won't know it."

Of those contractors still living and survivors of those who had been murdered, all were in Carsonville except one who had moved to Oregon.

First on the list was a run-down neighborhood filled with For Sale signs and streets littered with trash.

"This guy had a plumbing business," Jerry said. "I thought plumbers made enough money to live better than this."

The question was answered by a woman who looked very tired. She had dark bags under her eyes.

"Are you Mrs. Morse?" Katt said.

"She don't live here no more."

"Did she leave a forwarding address?"

"Last I heard her and the kids was livin' on the street."

What happened?"

"She couldn't even afford the rent on this dump."

"Do you know how we could find her?

"Drive around skid row. Look for a redhead with two little kids."

"Thanks," Katt said.

Back in the van, Jerry suggested they cruise the area near the soup kitchen, where many of the homeless congregated.

The soup kitchen and food bank were in the warehouse district, far from neighborhoods where there would be complaints from residents offended by dirty, smelly beggers on their streets.

"Redhead, two kids," Gary said.

A red haired woman would stand out in a sea of gray.

It didn't take long.

"There she is," Katt said.

Gary pulled over to the curb and Katt got out.

"Are you Mrs. Morse?

The woman looked startled, on guard for threats to herself and her children.

"I'm Muriel Morse. Who are you?"

"I'm Katt Li with TV News Seven."

She started to walk away.

"I don't want to talk to TV.

"No, no. That's not why we're here. It's about the loss of your business. We wanted to find out what happened to cause you to be living down here."

The woman thought about it for a moment, then decided the request was innocent enough.

"When Alex Tucker refused to pay what he owed, we were still stuck for all the materials we bought for the job. What he offered wouldn't even cover those costs. My husband refused to accept it and threatened to go to state officials. So Tucker declared bankruptcy and we got nothing. We went bankrupt ourselves and lost the business and the income that went with it. The stress was too much for my husband. He had a fatal heart attack. With only one income I couldn't keep up the house payments and I lost it. We ended up here."

Katt estimated the little girl was about six-years-old, and the boy about four. They skipped happily on the sidewalk and did not appear as emotionally affected by their circumstances as their mother.

A woman who looked as old as Muriel Morse would not have children the ages of the two running around the sidewalk. Worry had added years to her looks.

"Were you a working mom?"

"I was until I couldn't afford both child care and a place to live. We don't have any relatives we could go to. The few friends I have are not in a position to take us in. This was my only choice."

"Aren't there some programs that could have helped?"

"We had public assistance for awhile, but that ran out and here we are. Foster care wasn't a choice. I would sell my organs before I would put my kids in that system."

That got Katt's attention. She was starting to like this woman. Katt knew more than anyone the abuse foster children could suffer, having suffered it herself as a child.

"You're obviously no dummy," Jerry said. "Educated, I would guess."

The woman smiled. Rare given her current situation.

"U.C. Davis history major. I thought I might teach."

"Where do you go at night?"

"Our car was paid off, so we're lucky to have a relatively safe place to sleep. I don't have gas money."

"Are there other families like yours with working mothers out here?"

"I know of three in almost the same situation. Could be more I don't know about."

"If you had child care, could you go back to work?"

"I talked to my old boss and he said I could come back anytime. He doesn't know about us living out here like this."

"What if you could get the money you lost?"

"How could I do that? Tucker cheated us out of it."

"Do you still have a business bank account?" Katt said.

"Yes, I never bothered to close it. Why?"

"How much did Tucker owe you?" Katt said.

"Thirty-eight-thousand dollars."

"If you will trust me with the account numbers, you will find that Alex Tucker has paid your bill in full."

"How . . .?"

"We tapped into one of his accounts. But you must promise never to tell anyone how the money came to you. We would be in a lot of trouble if it got out. As far as anyone has to know, Alex will have paid what was owed."

"Ohmigod. I promise. Are you serious?"

She rummaged through a large tote. Katt saw a cell phone in the bag. Muriel tore off a deposit slip with the account numbers on it and handed it to Katt.

"Is your phone charged up?" Jerry said.

"Yes, the soup kitchen lets me recharge it there. I will lose the service at the end of this month. I can't afford the payment."

"You can now. Let me have your phone number. Watch your account," Katt said. "The money will be there as soon as the bank credits it."

"I can't believe it. You're not joking with me are you?

"Check your account tomorrow and see for yourself," Katt said.

"Thank you. If this is real you've saved my life. I've thought many times of shutting myself in the garage with the car. But I don't have a garage anymore. And I have my kids to think of. Now I can have child care and a place to live. For as long as the money lasts. It will get us going again until I can get back to making a living."

"We may have a low cost child care solution for you," Katt said. "It's something I'm working on."

"That would be wonderful."

"Do you have enough gas in your car to get you to a gas station?"

"I have about a quarter of a tank."

Katt had stopped at her bank and taken two thousand dollars out of her personal savings account in twenty-dollar bills. She never spent any money on herself beyond basic living expenses. What she had in mind was better than money gathering dust and puny interest in the bank.

Katt had Muriel and the children get into their car. She joined them there. So none of the other homeless could see, she gave the woman two-hundred dollars in twenties toward a tank of gas and lodging.

"That should get you a safe place for a couple of nights and some decent food until you can get to your bank money. I think you'll find the cheapest motels on the main highway. We'll be in touch," Katt said.

She left the awestruck woman and made a call.

They had not noticed, but a car had been following them and was parked about a block away.

"Gus, would you transfer some money to an account for me? I have the information.

"For you I would climb the highest mountain, swim the deepest ocean—"

"That is so sweet, Gus, but would you transfer forty-eight-thousand dollars out of my Cayman account?"

"Oh, sure, that too. A lot easier than climbing mountains and swimming oceans."

Katt gave Gus the account numbers. A few clicks of the keyboard later he said, *"done."*

"And, Gus," Katt said, "pay yourself fifty-thousand dollars as a consultant fee."

"Holy frijoles, I thought I was working for beer and for being on your short list."

"You deserve it, Shadowman. We couldn't have done any of this without you. I'll have more deposits to make today. Talk to you then."

Jerry was looking at the human misery all around them.

"I added ten-thousand dollars to what was owed," Katt said, "to partially make up for what this woman has gone through."

"You know, Katt, there's a story right here. We're due to turn one in anyway. Life is hard for street people. We should showcase that."

"Sounds good," Katt said.

"A lot of them hang around the soup kitchen at mid-day." Gary said. "One hot meal a day. Right here is the place to start."

The car that was following them moved a little closer.

A thin man approached Gary, who was holding his camera. The man's clothes were ragged and looked like they would fall apart if they were laundered. He was missing a few teeth. He appeared to have made life on the streets a career. He was pushing a grocery cart full of trash bags filled with soft drink and beer cans.

"You gonna take my picture?" he said."

"You want to be on television?" Jerry said.

"Yeah, what do I gotta do?"

"Just answer some questions," Gary said and turned on the camera.

"What's your name?" Jerry said.

"They call me Can Man 'cause I find cans to turn in for money."

"What do you spend your money on?"

"Oh, this and that."

"Would any of this or that include alcohol or drugs."

The man smelled of liquor in addition to not having bathed or changed clothes in quite some time.

"I like to have a sip now and then," he said.

Jerry asked a few more questions, then moved on to another man huddled in the corner of a building. His arms hugged himself as though he were cold.

"Can we talk to you for the TV news?" Jerry said.

He nodded, but looked afraid. He ran a hand over his face as though he were getting rid of a spider web.

"Are you ill?" Jerry said.

"Kinda. Need some medicine. You got a spare dollar or two?"

After they asked him a few questions about his life on the street, Gary slipped him two dollars.

"He'll just use it for drugs," Jerry said.

"I know, but he's suffering. My giving him money won't help in the long run. He's going to use drugs anyway, so all I can do is provide some comfort for now."

Gary's compassion was one of the many reasons Jerry loved the man.

Katt was looking for another interviewee when an engine roared behind them.

Gary turned to see a speeding car. Leaning out of the window of the car was Alex Tucker who was aiming a gun at them.

"Gun! Take cover."

Katt grabbed the handles on Jerry's chair and rolled him to relative safety with the van between them and the shooter.

Gary snatched his weapon out of his belt and shot at the car just as Tucker fired at him.

Both shots missed their intended target and the car sped away.

When to chaos settled down, they realized that Tucker's bullet had found a victim. The drug addict they just interviewed.

The man had been struck in the chest. Gary examined him for vitals and found none.

"Shit!"

Jerry called for an ambulance and police, for all the good it would do.

Katt checked with the group of homeless gathered around.

"Anybody else hurt?"

No one spoke up.

Gary got on his phone.

"Lou, Tucker shot at us just now on skid row."

"You hurt?"

"He missed us, but his shot killed a junkie we interviewed."

"We have him for murder now."

"Attempted murder on me, manslaughter on the innocent bystander, reckless endangerment, illegal discharge of a firearm within city limits."

"Close enough."

Gary gave Lou the location and a description of the car.

"So, he's still in Carsonville."

"I have a hunch he's only here for revenge. Now that he's blown it I think he will head for his hideout, wherever the hell that is. I'll call you when I find out anything."

"Watch your back. Alex may still be in the area. The group is meeting at the D.A's office in two hours.

"We should be finished at the station by then."

They stayed long enough to answer the police officer's questions. Then Gary called Gus and explained what happened.

"We've got to find Tucker, Gus," Gary said. "Can you do a search for all the properties he owns?"

"I will find the guy's hidey-hole if it takes me the entire rest of my lunch hour."

Gary could hear the clicking of a keyboard as Gus had already started his search.

"Never doubted it, Shadowman."

Gary got some video of the ambulance crew taking the unfortunate junkie away.

Team Jerry finished its interviews on the street and got plenty of B roll. One story had turned into two. Gary and Katt allowed themselves to be interviewed to say that it was Alex Tucker who shot at them, but the bullet killed the bystander instead. Gary explained briefly the reason they were the target. That story would make the nightly news.

For the homeless story, they interviewed managers and servers at the soup kitchen. Not everyone on the street was an addict or mentally ill. Circumstances had forced a lot of everyday people into homelessness. Most of those were too embarrassed to allow themselves to be interviewed.

The team returned to the TV station. They would have enough time to edit the video of the drug addict's death for airing on the evening news before they joined the gathering at the D.A's office.

The homeless story would run another night in the future. As they had been doing regularly, Jerry recorded two endings; one for the local market and one for network consideration.

When they finished, they drove to the D.A's office.

The meeting of the Ad Hoc Tucker Takedown Task Force was eager to hear the details of the skid row shooting.

"I figure Tucker went back to his hideout to wait for another chance to take us out," Gary said.

His cell phone rang.

"Shadowman, you're on speaker for the cops and District Attorney. Please give us good news."

"That's a big 'maybe' good buddy."

"Maybe?"

"It took me longer that I thought because I had to search surrounding counties. Among his properties, Tucker owns a cabin in the Sierra in his own name. If I were a betting man I'd put money on that place as his hideout."

"Do mountain cabins have addresses?"

"They didn't used to, but fire companies require an actual address for everyone now so they can find them if there's a fire. Unlike the old days when a plume of smoke was a pretty good clue."

Gus gave them the address.

"Google Maps shows what looks like an unpaved road to the place. There are a couple of cleared acres around the cabin for a fire break."

"Or a helicopter landing pad," Lou said.

"I'm sending you the coordinates."

"Thanks, Shadowman. When things settle down we'll get together and I'll give you the whole story. Meanwhile, check the newspaper and watch News Seven."

"Adios, amigo."

"Shadowman again?" Susan said.

"The Shadow can make a computer sing."

"Not always exactly legally," Lou said.

"We prefer the term 'extralegal'," Gary said. "We call him The Shadow because he stays invisible."

"So you're not a wizard after all," Susan said.

"The Team Jerry think tank is the wizard. It's the collective input of our entire group, you, Lou and Hank included. Seven heads are better than one."

"That's six heads."

"Shadowman."

"Oh, right."

"A police helicopter would be a sitting duck in that open field," Gary said. "Tucker always has ex special forces types working for him. You can bet he's got a sniper."

"Right. Ground troops it is," Lou said. "The cabin is in another jurisdiction, so I'll have to make a couple of calls to get an okay."

"The terrain would be too rough for you, Jerry," Gary said. "I'll call you on Face Time if there's cell reception."

Lou would order a fly-over to see if there was a helicopter at the cabin. He would have the police helicopter pilot stand by some distance from the cabin for a possible landing if they found what they were looking for and the place was secured.

After a short phone call, Lou said, "We have the go-ahead from the county cops. Saddle up."

"Oh, Lou I just love it when you speak cowboy," Gary said.

"You're lucky I'm letting you go along," Lou said as he dialed a call to set up the helicopter for a look at the cabin.

"May I remind you, Donut Boy, that you wouldn't be going anywhere without our investigation."

"Okay then, you can go along."

Susan looked at Katt.

"Do they always talk to each other this way," Susan said."

"Always. It's like two kids; oh yeah, yeah, oh yeah, yeah, my dad can beat up your dad."

"Lou was my partner when I was on the force," Gary said. "He's as much a brother as any blood brother has ever been. Same with Jerry, although I don't let Jerry insult me the way Lou does."

"No," Jerry said," I have my own ways to insult Gary."

Susan and Katt rolled their eyes and went to join the caravan.

Most of the trip to the cabin was on four-lane highway. The command car was in front, Hank Reynolds driving, Lou in the front seat; Katt, Gary, and Susan in back.

An armored vehicle with six SWAT officers brought up the rear.

"Some county sheriff's deputies will join us there," Lou said. "Our pilot says there is a helicopter on the ground and a car back among the trees."

"We don't want this guy to get away again," Gary said.

"The mayor is having a fit," Susan said. "He called and asked what we thought we were doing. I told him we were bringing a criminal to justice."

"We're also snuffing out the major contributor to his reelection campaigns," Gary said.

"He ordered me to stop the investigation," Susan said.

"Ordered you? What did you say to that?"

"I reminded him that the district attorney's office is elective, just like the mayor's. That puts my office far from his authority."

"There are those who might have said what we're doing is overkill for a grand larceny charge," Lou said. "Now that we have attempted murder and manslaughter, not even the mayor can argue with what we're doing."

"His Honor also wondered what will happen to the big development that was going to be such a boon to the city."

"Yeah," Katt said. "What is going to happen with that?"

"Dead for now," Gary said. "There is still that little pollution matter."

They turned onto a potholed blacktop road to the cabin.

"Gonna be rough from here," Hank said.

About a mile from the main road the bumpy macadam ended and it was rutted crushed shell-covered dirt from there.

When they arrived, Hank drove around the helicopter and parked their car so the aircraft was between them and the cabin.

"I wouldn't think they'd shoot through the chopper." Hank said.

SWAT drove the armored vehicle to the front. Men in military style armor, joined by county sheriff's deputies, surrounded the place.

The SWAT commander got on the bullhorn.

Gary was capturing it all on video.

"Attention in the cabin. You are surrounded. Come out with your hands up."

No immediate response.

"This is your last warning. If you don't come out in thirty seconds, we're coming in."

Fifteen seconds later the door to the cabin opened and one man came out with his hands up. It was not Alex Tucker.

"That's the guy who was driving the van with the guy Jerry and I shot," Gary said.

"Your testimony will be enough to hold him," Lou said. "While he's in jail we can work on proving whatever else he's been doing for Tucker."

Gary had to hold onto Katt because she wanted to punish the man who killed Alice Simms. She had some very ugly plans for him.

"Don't do anything now that will get him off on a technicality."

SWAT officers swarmed the man and placed him in handcuffs while others entered the cabin.

Moments later they came out, "Nobody here," the commander said.

"Are you sure about that?" Gary said as they approached the cabin.

"Where is Alex Tucker?" the SWAT commander said to the captive.

"Lawyer," he said.

Gary went inside and looked around. The others followed.

"We know that Alex always has escape plans," Gary said. "He had that secret stairway at his office. He has this cabin."

"Your point," Lou said.

"My point is that Tucker either has a way out of here, or he's still here."

"Where would he be," Lou said. "This is a pretty bare place."

Gary walked around. He checked for trap doors in the main room and a bedroom. He tapped on walls and stomped on floors. There was no attic, only bare rafters above with a hatch that opened to the roof.

Katt climbed into the rafters. "He wouldn't have come this way," Katt said. "A flabby city boy couldn't do it.'

She opened the hatch and looked out. It had no latch, so she just let gravity close it.

"Think, Lou," Gary said as he stood beside a blanket chest at the foot of one of the beds. "What in this place is big enough to hold a man?"

The trunk was not locked. Gary aimed his camera at the chest and flipped it on.

Hank and Lou were the first to take out their weapons. Some of the SWAT officers followed.

"All right, Tucker," Lou said. "Come on out. There are six guns aimed at you. If you have a weapon and show it, you will be shot. Come out right now with empty hands."

No response.

"Open the trunk," Gary said.

One of the officers lifted the lid.

"There's only blankets in the blanket chest," Lou said.

Gary wasn't convinced.

"That's a pretty big pile of blankets for just two beds, don't you think?"

"Lift the blankets," Lou said.

One of the officers pulled the blankets out. There, curled up in the fetal position, was Alex Tucker.

"Busted," Gary said. "Don't you get it yet, Alex? I will always find you.

SWAT cops threw back the lid and hauled him out with little regard for his comfort.

Gary got it on video.

Tucker glared at Gary as he was handcuffed. He was a bedraggled mess, a far cry from the neat, confident man they had seen at his news conference. Officers took him to the armored vehicle where his hired killer had already been secured. Tucker did not say another word. Not even "lawyer."

How did you know he was here?" Susan said.

"I knew Alex was a sneak, so it figured he would do something sneaky. Even if I had been wrong it was worth a more thorough search."

"My hero," Katt said.

"Okay," Lou said. "We got him. Let's see if we can keep him."

Gary stepped outside and found he had cell phone reception. He called Jerry on Face Time.

"Tell me you have him," Jerry said.

"Both Tucker and his thug," Gary said, turning the camera toward the two men in custody.

"And we lived happily ever after."

"Sorry you couldn't be here to see it but I have video."

"This is good. I'll get to see Tucker and the guy who killed Alice at their trials."

"We'll be back in an hour or so. See you then."

"Thanks for thinking of me."

"Always, brother."

Gary caught up with the entourage.

Lou radioed the circling police helicopter to land. The co-pilot flew Tucker's getaway chopper back to Carsonville.

"You may be a wizard after all Gary," Susan said. "We'll fast track his bail hearing."

"Not much chance of bail," Lou said.

"Depends on the judge," Gary said.

"Any judge who would release Tucker now would have to be an idiot," Susan said.

"I rest my case," Gary said. "Even if Tucker doesn't have any more money to pay off a judge, that judge would have to do what he's been doing all along or risk that Tucker would rat him out."

Considering Gary's stellar performance at finding Tucker in the trunk, no one would discount his judgment out of hand.

"If he gets bail, maybe you can insist on an ankle monitor, Susan," Lou said.

"A bought judge won't go for it," Gary said. "You'd have to put a tail on him."

"Not as easy as in the movies," Lou said. "But, as hard as it is for me to admit it, you could be right."

"His dad can beat up your dad," Katt said.

"Huh?"

"Never mind."

Susan chuckled.

"Wait a minute," Susan said. "You're all assuming he will get bail. It's possible everything could go perfectly smoothly."

Laughter all around.

Not only was Tucker not required to post bond, he was released on his own recognizance. However, his thug, now identified as Afghanistan Special Ops veteran Roger Shultz, would have to stay in jail until his trial and possibly forever after that.

"I made the strongest arguments I could that Alex was still a danger to Gary and a flight risk," Susan said. "He clearly demonstrated that when he fled to the cabin. The judge didn't buy it and didn't even require an ankle monitor."

"We'll take a look at that judge when this is over," Gary said. "It's practically an admission that he's on Tucker's payroll."

"I have some of my best people tailing Tucker on foot and in cars," Lou Wagner said.

Gary's cell phone rang. He answered and listened for a moment. "Thank you," he said and hung up.

Katt noticed that he looked very sad.

"What?"

"Lou, it's more important than ever that we hold onto Tucker and Shultz."

"Why?"

"That was the coroner. The report came back on the DNA tests. The blood on the car in the salvage yard is a match with Alice Simms, our spy in Tucker's office."

Katt turned away, not wanting them to see her tears.

"It's not admissible," Susan said. "Katt is not a sworn officer and she took the sample without a warrant."

"Let's say we get a warrant and legally connect the blood to Alice Simms and connect Tucker's fingerprints to the Ford," Gary said. "It's a short leap from Shultz to the man he worked for."

"Still no direct criminal tie to Tucker," Susan said.

"True, but that combined with the fact that Tucker diverted his parents' assets to himself could be interpreted as a pattern of criminal behavior and a possible motive for murder. Circumstantial."

"And the car the Tuckers died in," Susan said, "is in the same salvage yard as the car that hit Alice Simms."

"Plus, Shultz was one of the guys who tried to kill us. That didn't work out well."

"You're wondering if there is enough reason to believe Alex was the one who ordered Alice killed and if I could also get a warrant to look at the Tucker death car."

"Bingo."

"I'll check with my friendly judge and see if he will go for it."

She went back to her office.

Several hours later, Susan called Gary at the TV station.

"Got a warrant. The judge says if the Ford gave us the results we assured him it would he will give us another warrant for the Tucker Mercedes."

Team Jerry mouthed a silent cheer, fists in the air.

"Does Lou know?"

"He and Hank are on their way to the scrap yard with a forensic team. They'll take blood samples and check for fingerprints in the Ford."

"They already have Alice Simms' DNA results on record," Gary said. "But they will have to go through the same long process as before with the new blood sample from the Ford."

"We know the results will be the same."

"Yes. If we can keep tabs on Alex until we get those results, we can nail him and his thug."

"I'll let you know when I hear from forensics."

It wasn't long before Gary heard back from Susan.

"The prints in the Ford are a match with Shultz. He will never see sunshine again."

"He deserves more," Katt said. "Like maybe taken out along a country road and run down by a car."

"An eye for an eye. Somehow that seems appropriate in this case. But there is that darned old law thing."

"Shultz is linked to the Ford and he is tied to Tucker," Gary said. "Not to mention that Tucker made himself the sole beneficiary of the will. A motive for murder. That should be enough for a warrant to have a look at the Tucker Mercedes."

"We shall see."

THIRTY-TWO

Back in their editing booth mini headquarters, Team Jerry was enjoying something of a hiatus, with the final players in the Tucker saga either behind bars or under intense surveillance.

Katt said, "I want to get some kind of child care program set up for working mothers on the streets like Mrs. Morse and others."

"The place where Cheryl had been staying has some time left on the rent," Jerry said. "It's sitting empty now. We could offer it to one of those families until we can think of a child care option—maybe even extend it a month or so."

Katt got on the phone.

"Mrs. Morse, did you find a place?"

"We're in a motel until I can locate an apartment."

"You said there were other families like yours living on the streets. Can you put me in touch with any of them?"

"One in particular comes to mind. A nice woman with two little girls."

"How can I find them?"

"Her regular spot is about a block west of the soup kitchen. Her name is Abby Cassidy."

"I'll go find them right now. Thanks," Katt said.

"Not without us," Gary said.

They located the woman easily. She was the only one with two little girls about five and six years old at the location Muriel Morse told them about.

The woman was suspicious at first.

"Ms Cassidy, Muriel Morse said you could use some help."

Hearing Muriel's name, the woman relaxed.

Abby Cassidy was a frail woman who had to be in her early thirties. However, like Muriel, she looked older than her years.

Katt asked her a few questions about her background and how they came to be where they were.

Abby Cassidy's circumstances nearly mirrored those of Muriel's. She was a single mother. Unlike Muriel, Abby had an ex husband who was a deadbeat dad. She had been working, but couldn't be away from her children all day at a job without affordable child care and pay rent and living expenses at the same time. The Catch 22 put them on a street corner.

"Had you considered foster care?" Katt said.

"Not for one second," the woman said, becoming extremely agitated. "I can't believe you would even ask such a thing."

"It was a test question. I'm a veteran of the foster system and I don't recommend it for anyone."

"Sorry. My kids are everything to me."

"Lucky kids."

It was obvious to the team that this was a sweet young woman who deserved better than she got.

"We have a safe place for you and the girls until a permanent place can be found," Katt said.

The expression on Abby Cassidy's face was a mix of relief and caution."

"Really?"

She had obviously gotten her hopes up before, only to be disappointed.

Abby also had a car, such as it was, where they had been spending their nights. There was just enough fuel in it to get them to a gas station.

After the tank was filled they followed the van to the apartment.

The kids were much quieter than typical five and six-year-olds. They had learned that making noise attracted the wrong kind of attention. Even at their young age they had become street wise.

When they arrived, Katt explained something of the circumstances that caused them to rent the place. She gave them a brief orientation.

"Kids," Katt said, "it's important that you take care of this apartment. It's rented and the owners trusted us not to do any damage. I'm sure you will be respectful of the place."

They promised they would and their mother promised she would ensure that they did.

There was still some food in the refrigerator and pantry, but Katt gave Abby two-hundred dollars in twenties to stock up on the necessities.

"I haven't had a real bath in months," Abby said."I plan to take an hour shower."

"There's a washer and dryer in the utility room and enough detergent to last awhile."

"The washer will get quite a workout right away."

"Before the lease runs out we should have low-cost day care for the girls and let you get back to work."

"I can never repay you or thank you enough."

"No thanks needed. We can't solve all of your problems, Abby, but maybe this will give you a jump start until you can handle it on your own."

"I can find a job right away if I get someone to take care of the girls," she said. "I know of a couple of places looking for office help and I'm more than qualified. I have good references."

"If you're *more* than qualified, then you have been under-employed. You will need some good clothes for interviews. We can help with that."

Katt gave Abby another two-hundred dollars for job search clothes and for other immediate needs.

Before they left, Jerry asked Abby if she knew of two other working mothers in the same circumstances. She gave him names, descriptions, and likely locations.

"They're in a worse situation than we are," Abby said. "They don't have a car to sleep in and it's plenty dangerous on the streets. Especially at night."

They left the Cassidys to get settled and went looking for the other families.

They located the two women and their children and drove them to the same motel where Muriel Morse and her children were staying. They would be safe there for a few days until a more permanent arrangement could be worked out. Katt gave each some cash for food and essentials.

Katt convinced the motel owner that, since the average occupancy rate for motels was just 65-percent, that she should get a discount for bringing the rate up to 100-percent. She negotiated a weekly deal and paid the rent for all the families for a week.

"If things work out the way I think they will," Katt said, "there could be a better solution soon."

"Tucker would have a heart attack if he knew what we were doing with his money," Jerry said.

"Then we must be sure to tell him," Gary said.

When they got back to the TV station they put their heads together to think of where there might be space to set up a care facility and find reliable caregivers to staff it.

Gary called Gus to ask if he had any suggestions.

"I've been thinking of cleaning this place up,"

"It's a dump, Gus."

"I know. The city has been threatening to condemn it if I don't prettify it. If you fix it up you can have part of the bottom floor for child care. I'll rent out the rest of it once I have it rehabbed."

Gus's derelict would be put back into service after many years of disuse and deterioration. He could still live on the top floor and no one would ever know it. The first floor could be made to order for offices or storage.

"We'll pay the costs to remodel the child care space, Gus," Katt said.

"It's yours when you want it."

"If we get non-profit status you can use it as a tax write-off."

"The gift that keeps on giving."

Katt mentioned to Gus that if and when they could get non-profit status, she planned to buy a house or a duplex to use as transitional housing for families in situations like the Morses and the Cassidys.

Gus owned a modest house in a decent neighborhood that he used as a blind so the authorities would not know he lived well above his reported income level. But he never lived in it.

"You guys can use it for your rescues. It has to be cleaned up. I made it look like a bachelor pad; dirty dishes, clothes on the floor, the usual messy single guy stuff. I'll even pay the utilities."

"That does it, Gus," Katt said. "I'm moving you to the top of my short list. You'll be next if I ever dump Gary."

Gary and Jerry both laughed out loud.

"Eiiiiiii. How you feeling, Gary? Any serious health issues?"

"Feeling great, Gus," Gary said. "Katt will be a very old lady by the time your name comes up."

"Oh well, it's the thought that counts.

While contractors were working on the inside, others would create off-street parking on Gus's vacant lot and improve the entrance to the building. No longer would visitors have to enter through a flap in a chain link fence, walk over a rough dirt lot filled with trash, and crawl through glassless windows. The lot would become blacktopped parking. A proper fence would be installed with a solid security gate.

The room, itself, would be outfitted with a kitchenette, bathrooms, and laundry room. It would be divided into two classrooms to separate children by age groups.

Alex Tucker's ill-gotten gains would finally be put to good use.

Workers started to turn a shabby room with peeling walls and falling ceiling tiles into a pristine facility. It would be ready for occupancy in just two weeks.

"I've made it clear to the moms that they will have to pay a little something," Katt said. "People who get something for nothing don't value it."

"Only working parents below a certain income level would be eligible. Freeloaders need not apply," Gary said. "We're not providing a place for jobless moms to stash the kids so they can spend their days in a bar or gallivanting with boyfriends."

As Katt envisioned it, the center would rival even the most expensive care facilities in the city with its amenities for infants to pre-kindergarten. Local school districts are required to provide kindergarten for the older kids, paid for by the state.

Gus even replaced the rough plywood panel he had attached to the steel door to his upstairs quarters. When he wanted it to look like a slum he had painted gang-like graffiti on it. Now he would have a carved teak covering.

Katt had money transferred from the Cayman account to her local savings account so she would have cash for the project. She didn't waste any time finding other working mothers living on the street with kids.

The next order of business would be to find a capable day care administrator. Everything except homeless recruitment would be in the administrator's hands. Finding qualified moms would be up to Katt and Abby.

THIRTY-THREE

Katt, Gary, and Jerry drove to the funeral home to honor Alice Simms. Katt had ordered that the young woman be made as presentable as possible.

The viewing room was quieter than a typical room because of soft wall, floor, and ceiling coverings. The smell of dead flowers from previous viewings lingered in the air.

"She deserved the best we could do for her," Katt said.

Standing beside the casket, Katt, who seldom showed emotion, had tears running down her cheeks. Gary had an arm around her on one side, Jerry on the other.

"She looks pretty," Katt said. "She didn't deserve this."

"Not much consolation," Gary said, "but her killer is going to pay for it."

"It can never be enough," Katt said.

A burial plot and tombstone had been arranged for the young victim, all at Alex Tucker's expense.

"Susan told me they found Alice's application for the internship with Tucker. It didn't list any next of kin or emergency contact."

No one else showed up at the funeral home despite an obituary and a small story in the newspaper.

"No family, no friends," Katt said. "This shy little girl was completely alone in the world and they took everything she had from her."

Jerry and Gary knew there was nothing they could say that would make Katt's burden lighter, so they just held her until the tears stopped. Gary and Katt drove back to the TV station. Jerry went to Cheryl's.

Gary was in the newsroom when Lou called.

"Shultz has escaped,"

"What? How?"

"He was complaining of chest pains and was being taken to the hospital by two guards. He overpowered them. One is in pretty bad

shape with a head injury. The other one has some broken bones. They underestimated this guy's strength and training. He took their guns."

"Katt is gonna go ballistic. She already figured any punishment wouldn't be enough."

"Police are scouring the city, but it's a needle in a needle-stack."

"I'm going to have to break the news to her and it won't be pretty.

"I don't envy you," Lou said and hung up.

Gary dreaded telling Katt what happened, but it had to be done.

She was working at the computer when Gary returned to the booth.

"I have some bad news," Gary said, hoping to soften the blow.

"Just what I need. Tell me."

No way to say it but to say it, so he said, "Shultz has escaped."

Katt became as still as Gary had ever seen her, staring intently at him. Then, as though a volcano was bringing up disaster from its depths, she erupted.

She sprang from her chair. "I will find him and I will kill him," she screamed.

"*We* will find him," Gary said. "Let's approach this rationally.

"You be rational. I'm not capable of it right now."

Katt was so angry she was shaking.

"We have to think of places he would go."

"Do not . . . I repeat . . . do *not* bring Susan and Lou into this. I want him all for myself."

"Agreed. Now, where would you go if you were being hunted for murder?"

"Out of town, for sure."

"If it were me I would hide in a place where the cops already looked."

Katt went wide-eyed and nodded slowly. "The cabin."

"Worth checking. The police wouldn't think he was dumb enough to go back there."

"That would actually be a smart move."

Gary gathered up what they would need for the trip to Tucker's mountain hideout.

"How would he get there?" Katt said.

"Hot wire a car and head for the hills."

"Let's go," she said, and flew out the door ahead of Gary.

"He will never see me coming."

On the way to the foothills Gary called Jerry.

"Shultz escaped. We think he went to Tucker's cabin in the foothills. Katt and I are headed there now."

"Does Lou know?"

"No, and don't tell him or Susan. Katt wants the guy all to herself."

"Ah, man. I pity him. Almost. He'll be lucky if he comes out of this alive."

"It won't be pain free, that's for sure."

It was a quick trip, since they knew where they were going. When they got to within a hundred yards of the cabin they parked the van and walked through the woods to a spot on a rise above it. They could see that a 1990s Toyota Corolla was parked deep among the trees where it could not be seen from the air.

"You were right," Katt said. "He's here."

"He's here, has two handguns, and knows how to use them."

"What do you suggest?"

"You deserve your shot at him, but it's going to be risky."

"Worth it. You distract him. Get him to come outside to check on it. I'll climb through that roof hatch above the bedroom."

"Can you get up there without making noise?"

"You're joking, right?"

Indeed, Katt was well-named. She walked as softly as a feline. There was no danger that Shultz would hear her coming. Whether he would *see* her coming was Gary's job to prevent.

There was only one small window at the back of the cabin. The north side was the direction cold winter winds came from, so cabins were built with as few openings as possible on the windward side. All the large windows were on the south side to catch the warmth of the northern hemisphere's fall and winter sunshine.

Gary remembered from their previous visit the small window in the back was a bathroom. Small chance their approach would be noticed.

They walked carefully, trying not to make any sound that could warn the man inside.

"With the agility of a monkey, Katt scaled the back wall and crept silently across the roof. She turned to Gary and nodded.

With one hand Gary threw a rock against the end of the cabin nearest the door. The other hand held the Colt .45, a round in the chamber, safety off.

Gary walked around to the back of the building, out of view of the front porch. He heard the door open and heavy footsteps on the porch. He waved and nodded to Katt, who was standing by the roof hatch. She opened it carefully and disappeared into the bedroom end of the cabin.

Positioned in the rafters, Katt could see that the front door was still open and her prey had not yet come back inside. She shut the hatch carefully, lowered herself to the floor, and hid behind one of the beds.

The door closed and she heard footsteps on the wooden floor. They stopped somewhere around the kitchen.

She risked a peek and saw that he was facing away from her. She crept a little closer, hiding behind the other bed.

Another risk, another peek, another few feet closer.

Finally, she estimated that she could reach the man before he could react.

She sprang at him, covering the short distance to her target in less than two seconds and delivered a vicious kidney blow, sending him to his knees. At the same time she snatched the gun he had in his belt at his back and slid it toward the door.

"Gary!"

Gary burst through the door, gun aimed forward.

Shultz screamed in pain, but he was not without fighting skills of his own. He got to his feet and swung a meaty fist toward Katt's head. But her head no longer occupied that space. She snatched the second gun out of the front of the man's belt and slid it to Gary,

Schultz struggled to his feet. "You are quick," he said. "But you're no match for me."

"You won't find me as easy to kill as that poor girl you ran down with your car."

"That was fun. She made quite a splat on the grill. Ruined a good Ford. Now it's your turn."

Katt's anger went up a notch, but she knew she had to focus on putting this man out of action. Anger would make her less effective as a fighter.

"You're in the hummingbird weight class," he said. "I'm gonna pull out your feathers."

Before he could say another word, the hummingbird unloaded one-hundred pounds of pent-up fury on him. His crotch took a vicious kick. As he swung at her with no connection, she broke several of his ribs, his jaw, and pounded his face into raw meat.

"Broken ribs hurt, don't they, scum?"

Shultz was howling in pain, but she wasn't done with him yet.

From behind, she swept his legs out from under him, dislocating a knee. Her actions were a blur, too fast for Shultz to react. All he could do was receive the blows.

"Gary had seen a lot of savagery when he was a cop. He knew that what Katt had in mind for Schultz was far worse than anything he had ever experienced.

"Does it hurt yet, killer?"

"No more," he begged.

"Did Alice Simms beg for her life, scum?" Katt continued to pound him. She wedged his right arm between a roof support and the leg of one of the beds. She bent the limb to the breaking point. Gary could hear the bone snap from across the room.

"Please."

Then she did the same with his left leg. Shultz probably had not cried since he was a child.

"No mercy, you miserable excuse for a human being. Just like you showed no mercy for that young girl."

Then she executed a spinning kick to Shultz's head, knocking him to the floor, only half conscious.

"Gary, knife."

Gary reached into one of the pockets of his fishing vest, found his pocket knife and handed it to Katt.

She crashed two table lamps to the floor and cut the wires from them and tossed the knife back to Gary. She rolled Shultz onto his stomach, purposelessly dislocating a shoulder and used the wires to secure his hands and feet.

"Wake up killer," Katt said, slapping is face until she got his attention. "I want you awake for this."

"How about if I set this place on fire with you in it?"

"No! Kill me. Please."

"I promised myself that when we found you I would kill you, and it would be slow and painful and terrifying. I considered taking you out on a country road and running you down like you murdered Alice Simms."

Katt choked back a sob when she thought of what the man had done to the young girl.

"Watching you burn to death would be my second choice."

Shultz turned to Gary. "Kill me," he pleaded, barely able to get the words out with his broken jaw.

Gary was actually starting to feel a little sympathy for the man. But he knew that what Katt was doing would go a long way toward easing her guilt over recruiting Alice to join the investigation.

Katt stood back, hands on her hips, and looked at the man for what seemed like a long time. She turned slowly to Gary.

"I really want to kill him."

"He deserves it. Whatever you decide, I will support you."

Katt let out a long sigh and the tension seemed to leave her body.

"This is your lucky day, scum. Instead of a painful death today you will get to enjoy your life in prison. I hear that is worse than dying. You will have a long time to think about what you did to Alice."

"I'll get the van," Gary said.

"Hurry before I change my mind."

Gary picked up the guns Shultz had taken from the cops he injured as they were taking him to jail.

"I'll be back in ten minutes," Gary said and raced out the door.

"You won't be getting away this time," Katt said.

"Eat shit, bitch."

"Ah. You're trying to make me mad so I will kill you. Well, giving you what you want is the last thing I will do. I may break a few more bones, though. How about another dislocated shoulder?"

"No, please."

She did it anyway.

When Gary returned, they both picked Shultz up and carried him to the van. They tossed their prisoner into the back, ignoring his screams, all of which Gary caught on his buttonhole camera.

Gary called Jerry on Face Time to fill him in and to see the hogtied prisoner.

"Katt rearranged his facial features. Busted him up pretty good."

"You guys have all the fun and I'm stuck here."

"Sorry, pal. I did get some video for you though," Gary said. "It's too graphic to use on the air, but we can enjoy it on cold winter movie nights. We'll see you after we deliver this creep."

<u>THIRTY-FOUR</u>

We got Shultz, Lou," Gary said as they drove back to Carsonville.

"You what?"

"He was at the cabin. Katt beat him up and he's in the back of my van. Where do you want him?"

"Katt . . ."

". . . beat him up. You should have seen it. The man begged her to kill him."

Shultz moaned.

"Is that him? He's still alive?"

"Katt's humanity outweighed her need for vigilante justice."

"I would have killed the sonofabitch," homicide detective Lou Wagner said.

Oh, by the way, he will need medical treatment for broken ribs, cheekbones, teeth, and jaw, a dislocated knee, a broken arm and leg, and a couple of other fractured, sprained, dislocated, bruised, and punctured body parts. He'll need a new face, too. Maybe an eye."

"Damn!"

"That's what I said."

"Okay, meet me at Carsonville General. I'll have a couple of uniforms escort him to a holding area."

"We also have the guns he took from the last cops who escorted him."

"You don't also happen to have Tucker with you, do you?"

"No, I—aw shit. You didn't lose him did you?"

"When we went to pick him up, he wasn't in the house. Using a little Mansfield magic, I looked for an escape hatch."

"And . . ."

"And I found one. A tunnel led to a back yard garden shed. I figure he waited until after dark and got out that way."

"Crap. Can't you hold on to anyone?"

"Sorry, we don't have Gary Mansfield's superpowers. We are mere police, not civilian media weenies playing cop."

"You're welcome."

"You did good, buddy. See you when you get here."

As smooth as freeways are, there are occasional rough spots. Each bump brought moans and sobs from the back of the van all the way to the hospital.

"Holy shit," Lou Wagner said when they got to the hospital. "That is the most injured injured man I have ever seen."

"Take it semi-easy with him, fellas," Gary said to the officers assigned to escort Shultz to the prison ward. "We want him to live to go on trial."

"You think we should take it easy?" one of the cops said. "He put two of our guys in the hospital."

"Yes he did. And he will spend the rest of his life looking over his shoulder in the prison showers. That's worse than anything we could do to mister macho there."

The cop thought about it for a moment.

"Okay, I'm sold. But it will be a bumpy ride to holding."

"You have our blessing, my son," Gary said and made a priestly sign of the cross.

The tight restraints across Shultz's chest added to the pain of the broken ribs and he complained loudly. The more he moaned, the more the escorts jostled him, finding bumps where there were none.

Tucker's hired hand was never going anywhere ever again.

"Okay, Lou. Now we have to locate Tucker."

"You know, Gary, I'm not even going to protest. It wouldn't do any good. You would go looking for him even if I did object."

"Well, there you go."

"Katt, you showed remarkable restraint.

"You have no idea. But, Lou, if you lose him this time I will find him and the injuries you see here will seem like a minor scratch."

Lou considered what she had done to Shultz. He looked at her bloody knuckles and shivered at the thought of the fate that could await Tucker.

THIRTY-FIVE

Gary called ahead to let Jerry know Tucker was on the run again. Jerry was waiting for them in the editing booth when they arrived.

"What's our next move?"

"Let's brainstorm. Where would Tucker hide out?"

"I doubt that he has any friends that would help him," Katt said.

"Maybe one," Jerry said. "I got the impression that Kathy Rankin was more than his office sidekick."

"Do we know where she lives?"

Gary's phone rang.

"It's Susan."

"I heard you did some more magic."

"We found him and delivered him to Lou."

"Considering how many times Katt said she was going to kill him, I'm surprised he's still alive."

"Katt is surprised, too."

"Now for Tucker, Mr. Houdini."

"If you promise not to tell Lou right away, I'll tell you where he is. Jerry figured it out. Not definite, but we're pretty sure."

"If I didn't know that you have always delivered, I wouldn't be able to make that promise. How can I help?"

"Do you have Kathy Rankin's address?"

"Why . . .?"

"Jerry thinks there is a good chance he went to her for help and I agree."

Gary could hear Susan rustling through papers.

"Here it is,"

"He is not getting away again."

"Please be careful, Gary."

There was a trace of desperation in Susan's voice as she hung up.

"We'll have to go at night," Katt said.

It was just after dark when Team Jerry arrived at Rankin's tree-lined street. Her house was a two-story Cape Cod style structure with an attic and an attached garage. Much larger, more expensive, and in a better neighborhood than one might expect an office manager to afford.

"It's not certain Tucker is here," Jerry said.

"I think your guess is correct," Gary said.

Katt nodded.

There were very few lights on in the house.

Gary said, "If he's in there and decided to run for it, he could raise the garage door and be gone in seconds."

Jerry stationed himself in front of the garage.

Katt and Gary quietly circled the house, looking in windows to see if there was any activity inside, yet trying not to attract the attention of neighbors.

Jerry stayed on the sidewalk in front. He kept the Mustang .380 ready thinking the .45 might be excessive.

Rankin was preparing food in the kitchen. Someone called out to her. The voice was male, but Gary couldn't identify it. He climbed up on an air conditioning unit to get a better view just as Rankin looked up.

She saw him.

"Alex, get out of here. There are people outside."

Gary flipped his buttonhole camera on and ran to the street.

"Tucker is in there," he shouted to Katt, who was at the back of the house.

Gary got on his cell phone and called Lou.

"We found Tucker. He's at Kathy Rankin's home."

Gary gave him the address. He repeated it, hung up and joined Jerry on the sidewalk at the front of the house.

They heard the sound of an engine coming from inside the garage. The door started to rise.

A Jeep Wagoneer was pointed nose out.

"Oh, shit," Gary said.

Jerry decided he needed the Colt .45 after all. He brought it out and aimed it at the vehicle's grill. He couldn't tell who was driving, but whoever it was could certainly see that a gun was pointed at him—or her. The engine began to rev up and the Jeep started to move.

Jerry fired three shots into the grill. The Jeep would not have made it very far with holes in the radiator, but the driver lunged forward toward Jerry.

Gary saw that Jerry was about to be rammed. He grabbed the wheelchair's handles and yanked him out of the way by a thin margin.

The Jeep turned onto the street and sped forward. It only got about fifty-yards away before it chugged to a stop.

Gary ran toward the vehicle, with Jerry working his wheels as fast as he could, and Katt gaining on them both.

The driver continued to try to accelerate, but it wasn't working.

It was Tucker. He was out of the vehicle and starting to run, with Gary close behind.

Sirens—lots of sirens—coming closer.

The smell of gasoline was strong as Gary ran past the Jeep.

"Give it up Tucker," Gary shouted. "You're finished."

With no warning, Tucker spun halfway around and aimed a gun at Gary.

"Gary's police training kicked in and in a split second he raised his own weapon and fired twice into the fleeing man's torso. Tucker fell over backward, his gun clattering across the street.

When Gary reached the wounded man, Tucker gasped and said, "You should have minded your own business."

"Reporting on crime *is* my business," Gary said. "I do this for fun."

A half-dozen cruisers filled with cops had arrived. They surrounded Tucker, weapons drawn.

"There's his gun," Gary said, pointing to the side of the street where the semi-automatic had landed.

Lou Wagner joined the group.

"He tried to ram the Jeep into Jerry and to shoot me, Lou. I wanted to catch him alive, but he gave me no choice."

"He appears to still be alive," Lou said. "Can't you do anything right?"

Gary chuckled.

Lou had one of the uniforms call for an ambulance and a wrecker.

"How'd you stop the Jeep?"

"I didn't," Gary said. "Jerry did. He shot the radiator. I think he must have hit a fuel line or something because it only went a short distance."

"Where's the girlfriend," Lou said.

"She was at the house, but I wouldn't count on it now."

To everyone's surprise, Kathy Rankin had remained in her home.

"You will leave here this minute," she said.

Instead of leaving here this minute, Lou had her handcuffed.

"You are under arrest for harboring a fugitive," Lou said. "And anything else I can think of."

Susan Griffin had arrived and said, "If Detective Wagner can't come up with any more charges, I'm sure I can."

Rankin struggled against the handcuffs and protested all the way to a waiting squad car.

"I have done nothing wrong. I am Chief of Staff to the most powerful man in Carsonville."

"That was last week," Susan said. "Things are a little different this week. Alex Tucker is currently lying on the street with two bullets in his chest."

"He is permanently retired from the Most Powerful Man in Carsonville position," Lou said.

"Also from the 'Most Eligible Bachelor' position," Gary said. "Maybe you two can work out some kind of conjugal visitation arrangement. That is, of course, if he survives his wounds and if you can stay out of prison yourself."

Rankin continued to complain and sputter even as she was loaded into the cruiser

"That would seem to be the last of the mob," Lou said.

"How did you know where he was?" Susan said.

"Jerry's a magician, too," Gary said.

"Maybe someday you'll tell me the whole story."

"Ha," Katt said.

"In seven years."

"Why seven? Oh yeah. Statute of limitations. If you told me everything right now I'd have to arrest you."

"Me? I'm just a simple television news photographer."

"Actually, you are the most complex man I have ever known."

"You got that right," Katt said. "But when it comes right down to it, he's always on the side of the angels."

News Seven broke into regular programming to air the entire adventure; from the thug in the cabin to Tucker, wounded on the street. The report said only that Tucker had been shot trying to escape, not that Gary shot him. Team Jerry avoided thumping its collective chest, simply reporting the story as it unfolded. But it was obvious to everyone that they had done the legwork and caused big things to happen.

There were some questions about Kathy Rankin's future. Susan Griffin was sifting through the evidence to see what she could charge Tucker's right-hand woman with.

THIRTY-SIX

The next day the DNA results came back. The blood taken legally from the grill of the Ford was again, of course, a match to Alice Simms.

"Shultz to Tucker to the Mercedes," Gary said.

"Tinker to Evers to Chance," Lou said.

"I have no idea what you're talking about," Susan said.

"It's just guy stuff," Katt said. "Don't pay any attention to them."

Susan said, "I'll see if the judge is still in the mood to issue a warrant for the car Alex's parents died in based on a mountain of circumstantial evidence."

"While you're at it," Lou said. "You might see if you can get one on Tucker's woodland property to take soil samples."

Team Jerry went back to the TV station.

"We should get medical help for Lester," Gary said.

"But he's the one who dumped the toxics in Tucker's woods," Katt said.

"Yes, but in the end he did the right thing. I think we should get him to a doctor and see if anything can be done for him."

Katt and Jerry both nodded.

Gary got on the phone.

"Lester, all of Tucker's thugs are dead or in jail and Alex is about to be charged with enough crimes to keep him out of circulation for a long time, if not forever. You can relax now."

Gary heard Manning exhale.

"I don't think I'll completely relax until he's in prison."

"Do you still have that doctor who did your diagnosis?"

"I have him, but I can't afford him."

"Yes you can. Make an appointment and we'll take care of the bill for your treatment."

"You would do that for me after what I've done?"

"It's what you did after that. You were key to the start of the investigation and even to the end of it."

"I don't know how far along the cancer is."

"Then don't waste any time. Get to the doctor ASAP."

The relief in Manning's voice was evident even over the phone.

"I'll call right away."

"Let us know what you find out. Talk to you then."

Gary clicked off the phone. "You know, Lester is a pretty nice guy. Uncomplicated. He spent his early years in the military. When most young people were living normal lives, maturing, enjoying the illusion of safety in everyday life, he was in some of the world's most dangerous hot spots. He never knew anything different. Never had any experience in the real word or learned a trade or even believed he could do anything else."

"You know, Gary," Katt said, "For a tough ex cop you're a pretty soft guy."

"I learned it all from you."

That gave Katt pause, thinking of the violence she had rained down on Alice Simms' killer.

"I may have to learn a little softness from you," she said.

"Never have any regrets for what you did to Shultz. He deserved what he got and would never have been properly punished otherwise."

"No regrets. I'd do it again right now. It's just that I have to start giving everyday people a break. Growing up in foster homes made me suspicious of everyone. I have to lighten up. You've helped me a lot."

"I guess you could say we're good for each other."

"I'm never letting you go, partner."

"I'm never letting you let me go, partner."

"Well, I'll never let you let me let you go.

"My dad can beat up your dad," Gary said.

"Not if I find the sonofabitch first."

"So much for lightening up."

Alex Tucker was handcuffed to a bed in the hospital prison ward. He would not have to be present for a bail hearing. Gary's shots had not hit any vital organs. Doctors said his chances for recovery were good.

Gary called Susan.

"How can we find out which judge Tucker will draw for his bail hearing?"

"That won't be known until almost time to be in court."

"Is there any way Alex could find out in advance and buy the judge?"

"If he had someone in the Clerk of the Court's office on his payroll he could pretty much choose the one he wanted."

"Could you find out quietly who makes those assignments?"

"I think so, why?"

"Because we don't want the judge Alex chooses, we want one who can't be bought."

"Hmm."

"It's your turn to be the magician."

"I'll see what I can do."

Susan worked fast.

"The judge had already been assigned. It's the same one who let Tucker out on his own recognizance."

"Can we change judges?" Gary said.

"We don't have to. That judge is retiring today."

"That's quite a coincidence."

"Not at all. I just called him up, told him we knew he was on Alex Tucker's payroll and he had to retire immediately or be arrested."

"My god, you are even more devious than I am. I am a real fan, Ms Griffin."

"I'm thinking of what I could charge the judge with, since he is the one who let Tucker go without bail. I also got the clerk fired who makes those assignments. He will be facing some charges."

"By the time you're finished, city hall will be empty."

"Lou and I are looking at the mayor and police chief. Maybe a couple of high ranking cops."

"I love a good bloodbath. You're my kind of woman, Susan.""

"Don't start," she said and hung up.

Katt and Jerry were chuckling.

"She's seriously in love with you," Katt said.

"And I love her. Just not the way I love you."

"That's why I'm not jealous and not upset with Susan, because I love her, too. She's one of the finest people I have ever known. Susan loves you for the same reasons I do. Can't fault her for that."

"You know," Jerry said. "I was looking forward to being your neighbor in that empty apartment next to you guys, but I got a better offer."

"What could be better than having us as neighbors?" Katt said, knowing very well what was coming.

"Cheryl has asked me to move in with her."

"Had to happen," Gary said. "If ever there were two people made for each other, it's you two."

"She might hate me in a week and kick me out."

"Not a chance," Katt said. "You only met a short time ago, but I think you sized each other up within seconds of your first meeting. I never believed in love at first sight before. I do now."

"How did your parents take your leaving home?"

"Very well. I've mentioned occasionally that I would like to find my own place, so it didn't come as a complete surprise. They've done so much for me. They've put their own lives on hold to accommodate me. I think maybe, at some level, they're glad I'm moving on. Now they can travel and do some of the things they couldn't do with me in their way."

"What do they think about your moving in with a girl?" Katt said.

"My folks are liberal thinkers. They also realize that there is nothing about Cheryl's and my relationship that even the most dedicated prude would be concerned about."

Gary's phone rang.

"What's up, Lou?"

"The forensic team found slits in one of the power steering hoses on the Tucker Mercedes. If that failed, the driver would lose control. The original investigators missed it."

"That doesn't mean Junior did it." Gary said.

"So it won't get Alex the needle, but a good prosecutor could make a circumstantial case. And we happen to know a very good prosecutor. What we already have on him will get him a cell for the rest of his life."

"I'd vote for Pelican Bay, home of the worst of the worst. He might even find love there."

"He's so pretty, love would find him quickly." Katt said. "That's a fate worse than anything I could do to him."

"From what I've seen, I doubt that."

Gary wasn't so sure either.

THIRTY-SEVEN

*T*he lab results came back on the soil in Tucker's development
property, Hazardous materials of all kinds."

"Which we already knew, Lou," Gary said.

*"Yeah, but there was something we didn't know for sure. The
forensic crew found what looked like graves near the dump site.
They dug them up. Sure enough, some bodies were buried there."*

The case against Alex Tucker kept digging up more evidence.
Literally

"We suggested that a long time ago, but couldn't look into it
until now. Any IDs?"

*"One grave we're sure of is Vincent Noonan, the window guy.
There was a wallet with identification.*

"His wife knew he had to be dead."

Three recently buried. Big guys. Gunshot wounds."

"Joseph Carnahan, Melvin Gingrich, and the one Jerry and I
nailed."

Gary made a mental note to himself to drive by Mrs. Noonan's
home to let her know.

*"Some others are a year or more old. No IDs yet. Forensics is
using ground penetrating radar to see if there are more."*

"Check them against a list of people Tucker cheated."

Gary emailed him the names of the "disappeared" Lester
Manning had given them.

"What do you want to bet that when the unknowns are ID'd
they will have some business connection to Alex? This just gets
better and better. What does D.A. Susan have to say about it?"

*"She says it's still not provable that Tucker personally ordered
the killings."*

"Lou, we've got him on so many other charges we don't need
murder in the first."

"Yeah, but it would be nice to tie a big bow on it."

THIRTY-EIGHT

The Carsonville Bee had a front page story about Tucker's arrest on suspicion of a long list of crimes. Lots of use of the word "alleged." It quoted people who claimed to have been harmed by Tucker's cruel business practices. The piece mentioned that Tucker's office was shut down, all his employees were out of work, and some of them may also be in trouble. The article did not hesitate to report that Tucker was only rich on paper. Even if all charges were dropped, which was not possible, Alex Tucker was close to broke and his reputation was destroyed forever. The newspaper, without identifying News Seven, even gave credit to "a local television reporting team" for uncovering the evidence that launched the investigation.

"Once everything is proven," Jerry said, "it'll take the entire issue of the newspaper to report it all."

In the following days more bodies had turned up in Tucker's woods. All men. Nine, including Noonan and the three thugs. Two of the remaining five had IDs on them. All were quickly identified as having been Tucker's subcontractors. They were reported missing more than a year earlier. Each had a business that failed just before their disappearance.

"The coincidences are piling up, Lou," Gary said.

"You have to wonder why investigators didn't put Tucker and the missing people together."

"They were spaced out over time," Jerry said. "If they'd happened in the same week or month, somebody might have made the connection."

"Lou, we should discuss who is to be charged with what," Susan said,

"Alex: Grand larceny. Bullets from the gun found on Tucker the night Gary shot him matched the one that killed the junkie on skid row. Murder won't stick, so attempted murder on Gary and manslaughter for the junkie. Attempted manslaughter for trying to run over Jerry with the Jeep."

"Okay. Kathy Rankin is probably just as guilty as Tucker, but what proof do we have?"

"Nothing solid. Staffers hate her and are more than willing to rat her out, but they don't really know anything. Same for the receptionist."

Team Jerry got in touch with the murdered subcontractors' survivors. They were owed a total of 340-thousand dollars. Katt had Gus transfer the funds to each. Jerry had even tracked down the man who moved to Oregon.

"We'll put all the Tucker money to good use as we see the need," Katt said. "It wouldn't be right to keep any of it for ourselves. I don't trust the government to use it where it belongs."

"Lester Manning called," Gary said. "The doctors told him the cancer had not spread and there is a good chance they can remove it. He's scheduled for surgery."

"Alex Tucker should be told how helpful Lester has been," Katt said. "I know he will appreciate it. I also know he will go bat shit if we tell him."

"Then we must, by all means, pay him a visit and tell him."

<u>THIRTY-NINE</u>

With the accumulated proof of Tucker's crimes, it was easy to get a blanket warrant to search everything he owned.

Gary gave Lou the list of properties Gus had given them. Lou, in turn, went to work with Susan to build the case against Carsonville's deposed Leading Citizen.

The major contributors to Tucker's downfall gathered in the District Attorney's office.

"I have called you all here," Susan said, "to gloat."

"And," Lou Wagner said, "to showcase Gary Mansfield's poor marksmanship."

"Hey, I was running," Gary said. "It was night, and Tucker was wearing dark clothes."

"Any real police officer, which, by the way you are not one of anymore, would have emptied his gun on the guy."

"Lou, 45 caliber cartridges cost over a dollar each. I had a limited budget for Tucker."

"A little to your right and the city could have saved a lot of money on a trial,"

"Here we go again," Susan said.

"I feel as bad as you do about Alex's being in recovery," Gary said. "If it will make you feel any better I can go over there and finish the job."

"No, no," Susan said. "We are happy to have Mr. Tucker alive to be further humiliated."

"It's not enough to send Tucker to prison for a relatively few decades," Gary said. "I want him buried *under* the prison for life without parole."

"Maybe your wish is coming true," Lou said. "One of his warehouses we searched was filled with military grade weapons valued at over a million dollars. Here's the good part. They were stolen from a U.S Army armory in Nevada. Now we know where he was getting the money to stay afloat financially."

"That will get him federal time," Susan said. "But I would like to keep him in discomfort in our state prison for at least a few decades before the federal government gets him."

"No big-time defense lawyer would touch this case," Jerry said. "He doesn't have that kind of money."

"What good would a big name lawyer do anyway," Hank Reynolds said. "There wouldn't be a death penalty to deal for. There's no way Alex would get anything but life without parole if it goes to trial. What's an A-List lawyer gonna do for him that won't happen without one?"

He'll be stuck with a public defender who would be sure to recommend a guilty plea instead of a trial. Maybe he could make a deal to avoid San Quentin or Pelican Bay. But he still wouldn't be eligible for parole for a thousand years or so."

"It's too bad Kathy Rankin was released," Lou said.

"What? Are you shittin' me," Gary said. "When did that happen."

"This morning. The judge said Tucker had been turned loose, so he was not a fugitive. He was out on his own recognizance and was just visiting his girlfriend. The judge was kinda right about that, although he was on the take to let Tucker go in the first place."

"Incidentally, Gary," Hank said, "Tucker says you stole money from him."

"Shows how desperate he is. Inventing things to get himself off the hook,"

"Yeah," Katt said. "Any money he had should go to the subcontractors he gypped out of what was owed them."

The group went quiet for a moment, put two and two together, and Lou changed the subject.

When things settled down, Susan got Gary off to the side.

"You must introduce me to your magician sometime," Susan said.

"I'm afraid that can never happen, Madam District Attorney/"

"I can keep a secret."

"So can I, and one of the secrets I am obliged to keep is the identity of Shadowman."

"Could you arrange for me to talk to him on the phone? There's something I want to ask him."

"Maybe. I'll call him."

Gary stepped out into the hallway.

"Yo, Gus."

"Yo back atcha. How soon will this be wrapped up?"

"Pretty much right now, Gus. The trials, of course."

"Okay, let's celebrate. You can buy the beer."

"Gladly. But there is one thing you might do before that."

"Name it."

"It's something you may not want to do. The District Attorney wants to meet you."

There was no hesitation. *"No, man. Not possible."*

"That's what I told her. That's a shame because she's one of the most beautiful women I have ever known personally."

"Wait. In that case. Ieeeeee. No, I can't. I mean, she's the D.A., man."

"She thought maybe she could talk to you on the phone. She wants to ask you something."

"On your phone. She can't have my number."

"I'll set it up. She will only know you as 'Shadowman' or 'The Shadow'."

"Don't put it on Face Time. You know I can't say no to a beautiful woman, although plenty of them have said no to me. Why is that?"

Gary went back to Susan's office.

"Shadowman will talk to you on my phone. He doesn't want to give out his number."

"Fair enough. When?"

"Any time you say."

"Now?"

Gary escorted Susan into the hallway and called Gus.

"I have District Attorney Susan Griffin with me, Shadowman."

"Put her on."

"Shadowman, huh? What kind of work do you do in the shadows?"

"The kind that needs to be done, but people such as yourself may not be able to do."

"How about if I occasionally had a job for you that was beyond the capability of anyone available to me?"

"Is that code for illegal? Sounds like fun."

"Not illegal. Exactly. More like shortcuts; timesavers. You would be paid, of course."

"My fee is two-hundred dollars an hour, but for one of the most beautiful women Gary Mansfield has ever known personally I'll make it one-hundred. I work pretty fast, so it won't cost you much."

"How can I get in touch with you?"

"Only through Gary. Then I will call you."

Susan gave Gus her personal cell phone number, which very few had.

"Payment is to be made to Joseph B. Lowe."

Susan thought about that for a moment.

"Joe Blow?"

"At your service Ms D.A."

"Call me Susan."

"And you can call me . . . Shadowman."

"Almost had you there."

"I look forward to hearing from you, Susan."

"Until then, Shadowman."

Susan handed Gary his phone just as Katt came out into the hallway.

"You two canoodling out here?"

"We're waiting for you to make it a threesome," Susan said.

"The Shadow says he will work with Susan sometimes," Gary said.

"That's really something. He only works with people he trusts."

"I had a golden reference. Gary told Shadowman I was one of the most beautiful women he had ever known personally."

"Why, that silver-tongued devil."

"He wasn't going to do it until I told him that," Gary said. "You know he's a sucker for beautiful women."

They went back to Susan's office.

"We have decided collectively that this calls for a celebration," Lou said.

"We should have a big blowout for everyone who had a part in this case," Hank said.

"That would be quite a crowd," Katt said. "We'd have to rent a place."

"City Park has pavilions and barbecue grills," Jerry said.

Each of us should make a list of people who worked directly on this case," Gary said. "There will be a lot of repeats, but that's okay. I volunteer Katt to put it together."

News Seven had been airing regular updates on the evening news. Every angle of the Tucker case had been covered.

"We should involve Dennis and Will to do the updates," Katt said. Dennis Murphy and Will Jeffries were the reporters on the other two News Seven field reporting teams.

"Yeah," Jerry said. "We've been getting all the attention, but they're hard working and deserve some kudos."

Team Jerry asked Will and Dennis to do some standups and blurbs to be inserted throughout the day.

"Won't Hawkins object if he didn't assign it?" Dennis Murphy said.

"Ignore Hawkins. We have the authority from the GM."

When Gary put their final hour-long package together to wrap up the story of the Tucker Takedown, there would be nine people in the class photo, not just Team Jerry's three.

The other TV stations were rewriting what they heard on News Seven and reporting it as though they had it first-hand. Competing station executives had complained that News Seven was given priority treatment by police and special access that they had been denied. The D.A's office's answer was that they were not making the contributions to the investigation that News Seven was.

News Seven had become both the most loved and most hated news medium in Carsonville. Loved because the man now proven to be a monster had been put out of business; hated as jobs that would have been generated by Sierra Estates would not be forthcoming. The project was as dead as yesterday's lottery tickets.

The haters could not be persuaded of the impossibility of continuing the project on a property that was unlivable because of the chemicals in the soil. Their answer was that if the TV station had not nosed into Tucker's business the project would still be on track. It seems that logic was not welcome by those who have already made up their minds.

FORTY

A Beretta .22 caliber semi-automatic handgun fitted snugly into the bottom of Kathy Rankin's shoulder bag. If anyone wanted to examine the purse, there was a piece of cloth that matched the interior of the purse to cover the weapon. That and all the things normally found in a woman's handbag were piled on top of it.

Rankin mapped out an escape plan for her lover. She had to get Tucker out of the hospital.

Tucker wasn't in the best condition for physical activity, but he would be able to walk a short distance.

Rankin had rehearsed the plan in her head many times before arriving at the hospital.

She walked into Carsonville General like she belonged there. She went to the closet where hospital personnel kept their linens and scrubs. The door was not locked. She quickly found the items she was looking for, including a smock of the type hospital volunteers wore.

She had an empty plastic ten-ounce soft drink bottle. She had watched a YouTube video of a bottle being used as a sound suppressor. In tests in a field outside the city limits she found that it didn't really silence the shot, but it diminished the intensity somewhat and made it sound less like gunfire.

Rankin walked with confidence and no one challenged her.

Empty wheelchairs were always parked along the hallway. She chose one and pushed it to a stop next to Tucker's room.

"Good morning," she said cheerfully to the officer guarding Alex Tucker's room. "I have to change the patient's water."

The cop did a quick check of her purse, not really its contents closely. He handed it back to her and stepped aside to let her pass.

Tucker saw her, but did not react. Rankin went to the bedside stand, picked up the stainless steel water container and took it to the bathroom sink. Rather than fill it, she emptied it and dropped it to the floor with much clanging.

"Omigod," she yelled. "Officer!"

The cop came running. Rankin already had the Beretta in her right hand, out of sight, and the bottle placed over the muzzle when he rounded the corner to the bathroom.

He looked at the dropped metal container. Rankin walked up behind him and, without hesitation, aimed the gun at the base of his skull and pulled the trigger.

The cop collapsed, a .22 caliber bullet in his brain stem, dead in an instant.

The sound of the shot was lessened by the effect of the bottle and the fact that it had been fired in the bathroom, far from the door to the room. No one responded to the sound,

Rankin dragged the body all the way into the bathroom. She took his handcuff key and his Sig Saur semi-automatic handgun and extra magazines, put them in her bag, and pulled the door shut behind her.

She retrieved the chair from the hallway, rolled it next to Tucker's bed, removed his handcuffs and, with some effort, loaded him onto the chair. She sat a skullcap on his head like the ones surgeons wore in the operating room and put a pair of dark-framed glasses on him to further alter his appearance.

"Jeezus, Kathy. That was amazing," he said as she pushed him down the hallway.

"I have a car parked outside, near the first floor elevator."

Her greatest fear was that Tucker would be recognized, since he was a well-known public figure.

"Nod like you're sleeping," She said.

On the elevator she was able to shield him from the view of other passengers by placing her body between them and Tucker.

When they reached the ground floor, Rankin pushed the wheelchair the short distance from the elevator to the exit. She helped Tucker get into the waiting rental car. The wheelchair was abandoned by the door.

In seconds, they were gone and no one had missed them yet.

FORTY-ONE

As the celebrants in Susan's office were discussing their success, Lou Wagner's cell phone rang. He took it away from the group for privacy.

His free hand suddenly went to the top of his head. The look on his face was well past anger and still building.

Lou was quiet for a moment, listening to the caller. Then he clicked off the phone. Gary had seen the reaction from across the room and came to his friend's side.

"What's wrong, Lou?"

Lou took a deep breath and said, "Alex Tucker has escaped."

"Christ," Gary said, loud enough the draw the attention of everyone in the room. "How?"

Rather than repeat the story he called everyone over.

"Tucker has escaped from the hospital."

As soon as the outrage subsided, Lou said, "The cop guarding the room was killed. Single shot to the back of the head. Tucker was taken out of the building on a wheelchair. People remember seeing a volunteer women pushing an old man in a chair at about the same time they noticed there was no police officer at the door of Tucker's room. A wheelchair was found outside one of the exits."

"Who could have helped him?" Hank Reynolds said. "He has no money or friends that we know of."

"From the description of the woman, it sounds like Kathy Rankin," Lou said. "Remember, the judge let her go."

"I knew that was a mistake," Gary said.

"Detectives picked up a spent .22 caliber cartridge in the bathroom where the cop's body was found. Also, there was a plastic soft drink bottle with a hole in the bottom. Looks like a homemade silencer. They're both being checked for prints."

"Premeditated murder, waiting in ambush, and killing a cop," Hank said. "All capital offenses."

"She won't get bail when we catch her this time," Gary said.

Gary was working up a terrible rage. He looked at Katt and Jerry and they nodded. Team Jerry left for the TV station while the others split up to do their part toward finding Public Enemies Number One and Two.

Radio stations were repeating the story of the escape and urging listeners to be on the lookout. TV stations were using public service announcement breaks in regular programming to show pictures of Tucker and Rankin. Teams Dennis and Will were doing their part with live updates as Team Jerry fed the latest information to them.

The police had little hope they would be captured based on media reports. What the publicity would do, however, would be to drive the pair underground and limit their movements. But they couldn't stay out of sight forever.

Lou called Gary.

"Rankin's Jeep was inoperable, thanks to Jerry. We checked her Visa card and she rented a car that has not been turned in yet. There's also a corporate Visa credit card. I called Visa and told them it would be a good idea to put a stop on both cards."

"That may be the only buying power they had. Without credit cards they can't afford to get out of the city. Unless they have some cash we don't know about."

"Chances are real good they're still nearby."

Was the wheelchair also checked for fingerprints?"

"Yeah, and they found eight different sets . . ."

"Aw, crap."

". . . Including Tucker's and Rankin's. Hers were on record from when she applied for a federal secretarial job back in the early 90s."

"I'm gonna find them, Lou."

"You know, I really believe you will, Gary. But could I ask you to keep Hank and me in the loop.

"I'll try, Lou, but if we have to act fast there may not be time."

"We have a hell of a team here: your guys, Hank, me, and Susan. Plus a cadre of honest cops. We're kind of an unofficial task force."

"Don't forget Shadowman. Maybe we should keep it going after this is done."

Lou Wagner knew Shadowman was Gus Tovar. They were introduced when Team Jerry was investigating the Russian mob. But he thought it wiser to keep Gus's identity a secret, since both Gus and Gary wanted it that way. If the D.A. became aware of a crime Gus committed, even if it benefitted a case they were working, being the honest top law enforcement official, Susan might feel obligated to press charges. What she didn't know couldn't hurt Gus.

"Pretty handy to have the D.A. on speed dial. Cuts a lot of red tape. Keep your head down, buddy."

Gary went into a huddle with Katt and Jerry.

"Okay, where would a badly injured man and a homicidally protective girlfriend hide out?"

"No doubt he needs medical help," Jerry said. "Those bullet wounds could not have healed very much in the short time since he was shot."

"He can't go to a hospital or a legitimate doctor," Katt said. "Not even a veterinarian."

"Treating him herself doesn't seem like a good idea, but that may be their only choice," Jerry said.

While Katt and Jerry continued to consider where the fugitives had gone, Gary called the hospital to talk with the physician who treated Tucker.

"The doctor says Alex is fairly stable," Gary said. "But he is going to need antiseptics and regular changes of bandages. Both can be obtained off the shelf at any drugstore. He's already been pumped full of antibiotics. There's some pain to consider. Nothing over the counter would be a hundred-percent effective.

"Let's check drugstores," Jerry said. "We work our way out from the car rental place and see if anyone bought an unusual quantity of bandages and antiseptics recently."

They divided up the drugstores and started making calls, identifying themselves as Carsonville police investigators. Which was true, lacking only department sanction.

"Got something," Katt said. "The clerk at a CVS Pharmacy says a woman bought three 100 capsule bottles of 600 milligram Ibuprofen along with a large quantity of bandages and antiseptic cream. She paid with cash. The clerk said she must have looked at the customer strangely because the woman volunteered that it was for the Girl Scout camp's first aid kit."

"Girl Scouts, my ass," Gary said.

"They may be planning to get out of Carsonville," Katt said, "But Tucker wouldn't be in shape for a long trip. They have to be close to supplies and services. They'll stay in the city."

He's not going to be fit to travel for at least a week," Jerry said. "They'd have to hide the rental car and have a place to stay."

"We should start looking close to the drugstore and car rental agency and work our way outward."

While Team Jerry worked on the puzzle, Team Tucker had plans of its own.

Kathy Rankin had planned well. After all, organizing was a big part of her job at Tucker Development.

She disguised herself as best she could when she arranged for a place to hide the car until Tucker was strong enough to travel. They could also live there while time passed and the police search calmed down. She had found just the place.

She paid the rent with cash rather than credit cards that could be traced. Tucker had a cash stash for just such an emergency. The authorities would be looking for credit cards purchases. She had to have a credit card to rent a car. After that she put it away.

The hideout was not first class accommodations, but it had electricity and she had outfitted it with cots and folding chairs. Before she went to free Tucker she stocked the place with bottled water, a lamp, an electric hotplate, a coffeemaker, a saucepan, a folding table, and food for a week.

"They'll never find us here, honey. Nobody would ever think of this place."

"They can't go to a motel," Katt said.

"It won't be Rankin's place." Jerry said. "How about one of Tucker's rental properties?"

"Tucker's properties are the first places the cops would look," Gary said.

"You can be sure they wouldn't be living on the street like homeless," Katt said. "Princess Kathy would choose prison."

"Think," Gary said. "A house or apartment is just a box to keep the weather out. Other than those kinds of boxes, what others might two fugitives use as a hideout?"

"Tool sheds? Garages?

"You know," Katt said, "I heard about surfer bums who rented garages for cheap places to live in. They only worked enough to earn money for food and garage rent. Something like that?"

Gary's eyes went wide, as though a light bulb had gone off in his head.

"That's it," Gary said. "I know where they are. Sort of."

"Oh, good," Katt said. "Let's go sort of catch them."

"That sounds exciting," Jerry said. "A sort of manhunt."

Gary called Lou.

"Okay, you asked to be in the loop, Lou."

"I feel honored that you would include the police in police work."

"As well you should, rookie."

"What do you need?"

"The Team Jerry Think Tank came up with what I strongly feel is the hiding place of the deadly duo. They are in a self-storage unit somewhere in the city."

"You gotta be kidding. What makes you say that?"

"As Sherlock Holmes said: 'When you have eliminated all which is impossible, then whatever remains, however improbable, must be the truth'."

"What have you eliminated?"

"All traditional forms of shelter: apartments, condos, houses. Especially those owned by Tucker. They know you would be looking at those first. I believe they went to unconventional quarters that we would never think of. But we thought of it anyway."

"I'll put some of my guys on it. What do you think we should be looking for?"

"A woman who made arrangements for a unit large enough for at least two cars. She would have paid in cash. She would be wearing sunglasses and some kind of hat, but not one that would stand out. Something like a baseball cap."

"That's pretty specific. You don't happen to know her bra size, do you?"

"Thirty-six C."

Katt and Jerry both snorted.

"While you and Hank and your gang are out there protecting and serving and catching criminals and eating donuts and stuff, Jerry, Katt, and I have an errand to run."

As Lou assembled his detectives and uniforms, Team Jerry drove to Jean Noonan's home. There had been no answer when they phoned several times.

No answer at the door.

"I'm afraid it's a tossup whether Mrs. Noonan took our advice and went into hiding. Or not," Gary said.

"They didn't find her body in the woods," Jerry said. "Not yet anyway."

"People like her live in a bubble," Katt said. "They get so comfortable they can't imagine anything bad can happen. You tell somebody like that to duck and they look around to see why they should duck and they get hit in the head."

"Nothing we can do about it," Gary said. "We gave her our best advice. If she didn't take it, it's on her."

They were on their way to the TV station when Lou called.

"It pains me to say it, but you may be right just this once."

"You found them?"

"We think so. The manager of the self-storage facility on Grant Street says a woman wearing sunglasses and a baseball cap rented a double two days before Tucker escaped."

"Did he say what her bra size was?"

"He did not. That's why we're not positive it's them."

"We're on our way."

When Team Jerry arrived, a half-dozen police cruisers were parked outside the gate to the self-storage yard.

The facility was typical of its kind; long, low rows of pale yellow units of various widths with barn red garage doors that opened upward.

"Unit 205, down that middle aisle," Lou said.

Lou Wagner directed one of the cruisers to enter the yard and park about ten feet in front of the unit so a vehicle could not get out. The officers from the other cruisers walked quietly to the unit on foot.

Gary followed with his camera.

"Don't forget," Lou said, "They have the gun she took from the cop she killed and the .22 she used on him."

They gathered quietly around the front of the unit. There was no lock on the door.

Lou used a bullhorn.

"Ms Rankin, Mr. Tucker, there are a dozen guns aimed at you right now. There is no way you can escape, so come out with your hands up and we can end this peacefully."

"Hey, Tucker," Gary shouted. "It's Gary Mansfield. You didn't really think I wouldn't find you, did you?"

After waiting five minutes with no response, one of the officers standing to the side of the door, grabbed the hasp and started to raise it.

With no warning, shots were fired from inside. A round struck one of the officers in the chest. Everyone dove for cover.

The cop was wearing a vest. He gave the guys a thumbs-up. The steel door had slowed the bullet somewhat.

Gary recorded the scene as more shots were fired and more holes appeared in the metal. The cop who was opening the door continued to raise it despite several shots coming close to his hand.

When the door was fully open, Rankin was ejecting an empty magazine. Tucker had the .22 and was aiming it at Gary, who was getting it all on video.

"Mansfield, you sonofabitch . . ."

Before he could fire his weapon, Lou shot Tucker in his gun hand, sending the small Beretta clattering to the floor. Tucker screamed, his hand a bloody mess, destroyed by Lou's 9mm slug. He slumped down in his chair and howled in pain. Kathy Rankin, meanwhile, had a full magazine loaded and a cartridge in the chamber. She raised the Sig Saur, but never made the shot because six officers fired at her at once, knocking her off her feet. Dead before she hit the floor.

Gary looked at the damage Lou's bullet had done to Alex Tucker's hand. One finger was missing. The entire hand would have to be rebuilt if he ever expected to use it again.

"By God, Lou," Gary said. "That captain was right. You really can shoot a gun out of someone's hand."

"I was aiming for his heart."

"Okay, now I don't *ever* want to hear you say anything about my poor marksmanship."

"There they go again," Susan said.

"It never ends," Katt said.

A medic had wrapped Tucker's hand and slowed the bleeding until they could get him to the hospital prison ward. He was cuffed and dragged to a cruiser, yelling X-rated language all the way.

"You ruined my hand, you . . ." he screamed,.

"Consider yourself lucky I didn't turn Katt Li loose on you." Lou said.

Gary would have to put a lot of beeps on the sound track to cover up the obscenity spewing from Tucker's mouth.

"Hey, asshole," Gary shouted. "Watch your goddamn language. There are ladies here."

"He's more concerned about his hand than about losing his girlfriend," Katt said.

"Psychopaths don't care about anyone but themselves," Lou said. "He would have cared about her only as long as she was useful to him."

"Surprised that Rankin tried to shoot it out with the cops," Jerry said. "Even after she had been told there were six guns aimed at her."

"Suicide by cop," Gary said.

"Aw. Didn't want to live without her beau," Katt said. "Kinda romantic when you think about it. Sandra Bullock could play her part in the movie."

"No, I could never see Sandy as a bad guy," Gary said. "How about Katherine Heigl. Nobody likes her."

"What did Lou mean about turning Katt loose on Tucker?" Susan said.

"You hadn't heard what she did to Shultz?" Gary said. "Katt holds several black belts in a variety of martial arts. Shultz will be in recovery for six months after the beating he took at the cabin."

"So, Katt, there's more to that small package than meets the eye."

"I don't carry a weapon, so I became one," Katt said.

"Hey, Lou," Officer Bob Brunner called out from the storage unit. "Check this."

Lou went to see what the officer wanted.

"Here's something you don't see every day," Brunner said, opening up a grocery bag stuffed with cash. Most of it still in bank wrappers.

"It looks like a couple hundred grand."

"Thanks, Bob. Find something to lock it in and get it to evidence."

Susan saw the exchange.

"You trust the officer with all that money, Lou."

"Brunner is a genuine untouchable. He's what every cop should be. I would trust him with my teenage daughter."

"I didn't know you had a teenage daughter."

"I don't, but if I had one . . ."

Jerry did a standup with the scene of the shootout in the background. Team Jerry left the cops to their work and drove back to the TV station.

On the way, Jerry called Cheryl.

"Alex Tucker is in custody again and Kathy Rankin is dead."

"Are you all right?"

"I'm feeling the best I have in weeks. You're safe now. The security team's work is done."

"Say it again for Janet," Cheryl said and put it on the speaker.

"Your job is done, Janet. Tucker is on his way back to jail and Rankin is dead. All clear."

"She wants to talk to you."

"Put her on."

"All clear, huh?"

"Tucker and Rankin tried to shoot it out at their hideout. It didn't work out for either of them. She's dead, he's on his way to the hospital and prison, his last remaining thug will be lucky if he can walk without a limp for the rest of his life."

"Sorry I missed it. I'll help Cheryl move back to her house off the clock before I leave. Frank's here. Gratis, by the way. He'll help, too."

"You guys are the best, Janet."

"Damn right. And don't forget, you owe me a 1911."

She handed the phone back to Cheryl.

"When will I see you?"

"As soon as we put the package together for the evening news. It's going to take awhile because it's a long one."

"See you then."

The entire newsroom staff was there to greet them. The day shift stayed after hours to help celebrate their victory. Except Stan Hawkins. They would not have expected Hawkins to join in.

Cyrus Weaver congratulated the team. "I'm approving bonuses and extra vacation time for the three of you.

"Much appreciated," Gary said, "but we would have done it for free."

"Quiet, dummy," Katt said and whacked Gary on the arm.

They all laughed.

"Where's Hawkins?" Gary said.

"Stan Hawkins doesn't work here anymore," Weaver said.

High pinkies all around.

They excused themselves from the festivities to put together the report.

"We should give Teams Dennis and Will a bonus equal to what Weaver gave us," Katt said.

"Even more," Jerry said. "Because they didn't get the extra vacation time."

By the time Team Jerry had finished putting its report together Team Janet was finishing up the job of moving Cheryl back to her house.

In the time she was gone, workers had patched up the damage from the grenade.

Gary had made calls to get the phone lines redirected to Cheryl's residence so she could resume her business the next day without a hitch.

"It's good to be home again," Cheryl said.

"You should never have had to leave," Jerry said.

"Janet, Frank, we've been talking about a bash to celebrate ridding the world of Alex Tucker," Gary said. "You and everyone at Anderson Security will be on the guest list."

"Say when and where and we're there."

"Meanwhile," Cheryl said, "you both have an open invitation here. If you ever get hungry or lonely, think of this as your second home."

FORTY-TWO

When Cheryl and Jerry were finally alone, they had a chance to talk about some things both had on their minds, but had never gotten around to discussing.

"I love you, Jerry Harper."

"I love you, Cheryl Whistler."

"Odd to say that when we've only known each other for such a short time," Cheryl said. "But I know it's true."

"It's much more than just understanding what it's like to live in a wheelchair," Jerry said. "We've talked about everything. You know all of my bad habits. You, of course, are perfect in every way."

"Of course."

They both laughed.

"I think too many couples don't get to know each other well enough before they commit to spending a lifetime together," Cheryl said. "We have time to work on it."

"That's what happened with Katt and Gary. They worked together for three years before they even considered becoming a couple. They talked about everything, told each other everything about themselves. By the time they got together they knew all there was to know. I know from the very start that you and I care about each other for all the right reasons."

"In the spirit of full disclosure," Cheryl said, "my parents were Republicans."

"I forgive you. See how easy that was."

"It would be nice to make love," Cheryl said, looking into Jerry's eyes as they held hands. "It would be great to have children."

"Lots of kids out there who need parents. Nothing says people have to make their own."

They held hands as they talked.

"I think too many people marry for sex and call it love," Jerry said. "When the sex cools off and each learns the failings and bad habits of the other, unpleasant discoveries are made; disappointments pile up, and there goes the relationship."

"I was young and a virgin when I had my accident," Cheryl said.

"I was, too. At that age, all I thought about was girls and sex. I spent my entire high school career trying to look up Patty Sweeney's skirt."

Cheryl burst out laughing.

"Any success?" she said, laughing so hard she was barely able to get the words out.

"Not even once."

Which made her laugh all the harder and Jerry laughed at her laughter.

Whether because of Jerry's story or from relief that their ordeal was over, it seemed they might never be able to stop laughing. Every time either of them thought of it, the laughter came again.

"I haven't laughed this much since maybe ever," Cheryl said, wiping tears from her cheeks.

"Me too."

"I was a typical boy crazy teenager," Cheryl said. "Funny how a person's priorities change as they get older. I'm sure that would have happened even if I hadn't been injured."

"Gary told me it was obvious to him that we weren't attracted to each other just because we were both in wheelchairs. Not because our choices are limited. We would have been a match even if both had been able-bodied."

"We can make a life, Jerry. It just won't be like everyone else's life."

They talked until late that night, staying close and holding hands.

FORTY-THREE

Team Jerry, Lou Wagner and Hank Reynolds met in Susan Griffin's office.

"The mayor's press conference was interesting," Lou said.

"How did he put it?" Gary said. "My administration can add one more success to its achievements. We have rid our city of a cancer."

"Nice try," Jerry said. "As I recall, Hizzoner fought us all the way. Now his administration is the hero? We'll see about that."

"I wonder how he will feel if I charge him with aiding and abetting?" Susan said.

"And his buddy, the police chief," Hank said. "I hate it when a cop is dirty, but the chief deserves the public shaming he's about to get."

"They would get off if it went to trial, of course," Lou said. "The mayor will claim any money he got from Tucker was campaign contributions. The chief will say he was following the mayor's lawful orders and our investigation was not officially sanctioned. But the stink would stay with them."

"They both put a lot of pressure on us to stop the investigation," Gary said.

"I think I'll offer them the choice of being charged if they don't resign or retire," Susan said. "Even though it's doubtful I could get a conviction and they know it, I think they'll quit. Especially after I hold a news conference and tell the true story of their obstruction."

"Lawyers would cost them all the money Tucker paid them," Katt said. "And their careers would be in the dumpster anyway."

"This is just one more reason why I quit the police force," Gary said. "There is no way we could have pulled off an investigation of Tucker if I'd still been on the job."

"Yeah," Lou said. "Following the law is such a bother."

"What do you mean? We didn't break any laws."

"You sure put a dent in some of them," Susan said.

"The road to justice is a bumpy one," Katt said.

"What will happen to Tucker?" Jerry said.

"It will cost the city a fortune to try him," Susan said. "But I don't want him to plead guilty for the possibility of parole some day. I will ask the judge to refuse to accept a plea deal even before Tucker has a chance enter a guilty plea. I want him to get the maximum sentence in the toughest prison for whatever we're able to charge him with."

"If he ever gets out," Gary said, "a few more laws are going to get dented."

FORTY-FOUR

It was after dark when the party got started. Katt had arranged for a pavilion in City Park for a get-together with everyone who played a role in taking down Alex Tucker. The event attracted some street people. But no one was turned away. Katt still had a pocket full of twenties and she slipped quite a few to the homeless.

The place was alive with Lou's personal cop corps out of uniform, security people from Pat Anderson's outfit, and practically the entire district attorney's office staff.

Everyone stood around talking about the various aspects of the case and their part in it. Those who had only parts of the story were filled in on the rest.

"Officer Brunner, . . . Bob," Gary said. "I want to thank you for all your help."

"Any time. I didn't find out until yesterday that it was related to the Tucker case."

"We had to keep a lid on what we were doing for fear it could get back to Tucker. One of the guys you were checking up on is right over there. And the young lady where the grenade was thrown through the window is over there."

"I like you guys' style. If you ever need an assist in the future, I'm in. On or off duty."

Lester Manning was introduced around as the guy who got the ball rolling in the case.

"Some people are going to prison because of you, Lester," Gary said.

"I was sure I was a dead man," Manning said. "If not killed by Tucker's goons, then by the cancer. When I was a kid and you heard someone had cancer, it meant they were dying."

"There are several hundred types of cancers and quite a few of them can be cured or controlled these days."

Gary introduced Lester Manning to Lou Wagner and Hank Reynolds.

"You know, Lester," Lou said, "from what Gary tells me, the police department could use a guy like you."

"Me? I never thought of being a cop. In a way, what I did as a Seal was kind of police work. The main difference was that we didn't arrest people, we killed them."

"Yeah," Lou said, "you'd have to dial that back some, but why don't you think about it."

"The pay's not bad," Gary said. "Not without danger, but it's a job where you can look in the mirror when you shave and see someone doing good."

Lester said he would think about it, but Gary sensed that he had already made up his mind to look into it.

Drinks of the soft variety were in tubs filled with ice. Guests fished out their own. A caterer supplied a variety of finger foods.

"Hey, Gary," Gus Tovar said. "There's no beer."

"Park rules, Gustov."

"What kind of party doesn't have beer?"

Susan Griffin heard the exchange and said, "no alcohol. It cuts down on rowdy behavior and violence."

"I don't need beer to make me rowdy," Gus said.

"Have you met our District Attorney?" Gary said.

"Haven't had the pleasure," Gus said, shaking her hand.

"Susan Griffin, Gus Tovar."

"Are you sure we haven't met, Gus?"

"Definitely not. I keep excellent records of beautiful blondes I have met."

Susan laughed, but looked unconvinced. If she suspected anything, she kept it to herself.

Lou Wagner and Hank Reynolds hung around where Team Jerry was holding court.

"Gary, you oughta come back to the cops and work for us."

"I already work for you, Lou. I just don't do it with a gun to my head. Anytime you need me I'm there. We never would have been able to do half of what we did in this case if I were back on the force."

Gary knew that Lou knew what his answer would be. He just liked to give him a hard time.

Katt's cell phone rang. She was tempted not to answer it, but remembered another time she had not checked her phone messages, so she clicked on.

"Ms Li. This is Jean Noonan."

"Mrs. Noonan. You're alive. We went by your house and I called several times. When nobody was there we were afraid Tucker's man got to you."

"No, I took your advice and went to stay with my sister in Minneapolis. I forgot to take my phone charger, so I didn't get messages until I got back. I heard on the news that Mr. Tucker was in jail, so I came home."

"I'm relieved that you are all right. Thanks for letting me know."

"And thank you again for what you've done. I've lost Vincent, but I can get a new start because of your help. I was notified that his body had been found. Now I can give him a proper burial."

"Our condolences. Are you going to be okay financially?"

"Oh, yes. Vincent had a life insurance policy I didn't know about. That and the money you gave me is enough to reopen the business. I called all of our employees and they're anxious to get it going again."

"Good luck in your new life," Katt said and clicked off.

"That was Jean Noonan," Katt said.

"Another happy ending," Gary said.

The highlight of the evening was when Susan Griffin was introduced to Anderson Security owner Pat Anderson. Sparks flew in both directions immediately. Everyone present could see there was a couple in the making. Neither spoke to anyone else the rest of the evening and they were never more than inches apart the entire time.

Katt in particular noticed that Susan had stars in her eyes.

"Well, Gary, it looks like you just lost one of the most beautiful women you have ever known personally."

"That's okay. I still have *the* most beautiful woman I have ever known personally. Who also happens to also be funny and smart."

"And has the ability to kick the livin' crap out of you if you look sideways at another woman except Susan. She's pre-approved."

"I always thought your eyes were blue," Gary said. "But they are actually green."

Katt put her arms around Gary as far as they would reach. It was like Tinkerbell hugging a redwood.

Gus Tovar was introduced to Janet Mohn. They seemed to be hitting it off more than a simple 'howdy do' would suggest.

Frank was working the crowd, checking out the female population.

Janet was nearly unrecognizable in tight jeans and a XXL Black Sabbath heavy metal T-shirt instead of her usual ready-for-war garb.

"I don't know where Janet would stash a weapon," Jerry whispered, "but I'm sure there's one on her somewhere."

"I'm officially making her my sibling," Cheryl said. "I always wanted a big sister."

"What's a girl got to do to get a beer around here?" Janet said.

"I was wondering the same thing," Gus said. "What kind of party doesn't have beer?"

"Yeah," Janet said. "Hey, you want to get outta here?"

"We could go to my place?" Gus said. "I've got eight cases of Dos Equis, two of them on ice."

"That's a good start. Might be enough for tonight," Janet said. "I'll follow you,"

They left without so much as a wave.

"Omigod," Gary said. "I don't know if Gus can survive a night with Janet."

"We have to do something special for Janet and Frank," Katt said.

"How about an all-expense paid European vacation for two for each of them," Jerry said

"Or we could ask them what their wildest dream is and make it come true."

Janet had always wanted remote land where she and friends could shoot their guns, far from the ears of objecting neighbors.

Done.

Frank's dream was to own waterfront property to build a fish camp when he retired. Maybe add rental cabins and a beer bar some day.

Done.

It seemed that some other people's dreams were also coming true. Muriel Morse and Abby Cassidy were off the street and back to the life they both deserved; jobs, a place to live, and child care they could afford. Others were getting help, as well.

All made possible by the Alice Simms Day Care Center.

FORTY-FIVE

I'm going to bring Tucker's money back to the U.S. and make more money with it," Katt said. "I'll have to start a company to put it in. Something like Shadow Investments. Also, a foundation to distribute it, including our investigations. Some of what's left of Tucker's millions will get us started, but we're going to need money to keep doing what we've been doing. The police department isn't going to fund us or back us up in any official way. Even with Cyrus Weaver's moral support the TV station doesn't have the budget for what we're planning. So I want to get a good slush fund going."

Katt had proven herself capable of building wealth, although she required very little for herself. She didn't even spend much of her News Seven salary. Her only interest in money was as a challenge—a game; one which she was very good at playing. Much like her approach to poker. Blood sport.

FORTY-SIX

H ey guys," Jerry said when he rolled into the newsroom. "I could be leaving you soon."

That got Katt and Gary's attention big time.

"What?" they said almost at once.

"Yeah, I got a job offer from the network. They saw the shoe kid and Tucker pieces we sent them and they made an offer. Big money, travel, lots of perks including box seats at ballgames. A sweet deal."

His teammates looked pained.

Katt was first to speak.

"You deserve it, Jerry. It's a real career break for you."

"I don't know what we'll do without you," Gary said.

"Well, you don't have to worry about it," Jerry said. "I turned them down."

"Wha—are you nuts?" Gary said.

"I must be to work with you two dingdongs. They wouldn't let me carry a gun and shoot people, so that was the deal breaker."

"A network job is every reporter's dream," Katt said.

"It's not my dream. I'm living mine right now. I have a wonderful life here and I don't ever want it to change. Cheryl's here, you guys are here, my happiness is here. No amount of money could get me to leave."

Katt pounded lightly on Jerry's chest.

"Do. Not. Ever. Scare. Us. Like. That. Again, Jerry. Harper. You almost gave me a heart attack."

Jerry was smiling, but a tear rolled down his cheek.

"You are my family. I love you both."

"Maybe Gary and I could adopt you and Cheryl and make you officially our children."

"Absolutely not," Jerry said. "That would make Cheryl my sister and that would be weird."

FORTY-SEVEN

The Midland Development Corporation, a large eastern property developer, learned of the problems with the proposed Sierra Estates development and its collapse with the destruction of Alex Tucker's empire. They had gotten a tip from an anonymous source and sent representatives to research the possibilities.

Before the anonymous tipster made that call she bought a ton of the publically-traded company's stock.

The developer looked into buying the property and continuing the project. Alex Tucker may have been a criminal, but he had a great idea.

There was that hazardous waste dumpsite to contend with, of course. The U.S. Environmental Protection Agency declared it not quite a superfund site, but worthy of some funds for removal of a couple of acres of soil. The dirt would be hauled away in barrels for proper burial in a leak-proof final resting place. No wells would be drilled on the property because there could still be some risk of contaminants getting into the water table. All water for human consumption would come to the development through the Carsonville system.

Once cleaned, the huge hole in the ground would become a lake with water piped in from a mountain creek.

Any money left over from the sale of Tucker's properties would be applied to the costs of disposal and the feds would eat the balance if there was one.

The developers were able to purchase the two thousand acres for a song. With some modifications they committed to constructing practically a duplicate of Tucker's plan. They would even keep the name, Sierra Estates.

County and city tax breaks were incentives for resuming the project where Tucker left off. The architects and engineers had already been paid for their artistic and structural work. All the new company had to do was move in and paint by the numbers.

Katt had Gus shut down the two offshore Tucker accounts before federal investigators could discover them. The feds never learned of the existence of Tucker's millions.

Gary did happen to mention to Detectives Lou Wagner and Hank Reynolds, and District Attorney Susan Griffin that any unsanctioned future investigations by the newly-created *Shadow Force* would be very well funded.

<u>THANKS</u>

Special thanks to retired Pinellas County Florida Sheriff Captain Tim Ingold for helping me understand law enforcement procedures and tactics. Thanks also to fellow authors Dart Humeston and Mark Barie for their advice in the creation of this book.

As always, thanks to my wife, Sherry, for her patience during my hibernation.

www.ingramcontent.com/pod-product-compliance
Lightning Source LLC
Chambersburg PA
CBHW051951150726
47999CB00004B/1341